Sixpence in Her Shoe

and other stories

Maura Treacy

POOLBEG PRESS: DUBLIN

This collection first published 1977 by
Poolbeg Press Ltd., Knocksedan House,
Swords, Co. Dublin, Ireland.

Printed by Cahill (1976) Limited, East Wall Road, Dublin 3.

Contents

The generous assistance of An Chomhairle Ealaíon (The Arts Council) and of the Northern Ireland Arts Council in the publication of this book is gratefully acknowledged.

Some of these stories were first published in *New Irish Writing* *(The Irish Press).* "Separate Ways" was first published in *Best Irish Short Stories* (Paul Elek). "The Weight of the World" won the 1974 Writers' Week in Listowel Short Story Competition.

A Time For Growing

SHE HAD never been out so early before and her head was still full of sleep and when she looked up again Monica and Shem had gone on a long way in front of her. She began to run to keep up with them and she struck her toe against a sharp stone that was bedded in the road at the foot of the hill. As she scrambled to her feet, rubbing the grit out of her knees and the palms of her hands, she glanced resentfully at the stone. She saw it everyday and knew exactly where it was and she would walk in a wide circle around it or else step deliberately on top of it: the days when it didn't trip her now linked together in a strengthening chain of self-sufficiency.

The black bars of the railway gate were ice-cold as she climbed out between them. She glanced up at the shuttered windows of the lodge, recalling the downy warmth of her own bed. Then she ran on until she kept up with Monica and Shem; they were silent onow, submerged in their own thoughts. She walked on the rail, her arms held out to balance herself, her body swaying slightly as she moved forward; she stumbled, skinning the inner side of her ankle on the rail, and as she climbed up again, Monica grabbed her arm.

"Walk on the sleepers. If you break a leg today we won't have time to mend it."

There wasn't room across for three of them between the rails so she fell into step behind them: right foot on this sleeper, left foot on the next, then right again, making a small skip of a step where, at the joinings of the rail, two sleepers came close together. Sometimes someone over-reached or didn't reach far enough and a foot scudded against the pile of rough stones between the sleepers and the sound reverberated along the rails in the

5

empty stillness of the morning, impinging on her mind which still spun mistily with sleep; but the regular fall of their feet carried on unbroken.

She watched the stride of their legs. Shem's wellingtons were streaked with mud along the inner sides where they brushed against each other and the legs of his trousers were stuffed down into them. Monica, because she thought she might meet someone on the way, was wearing sandals and her legs were white; her wellingtons were in the shopping bag, folded up in newspaper under the flasks and cups and the parcel of sandwiches.

"You're making an early start," an old woman's voice called to them, and Miriam, startled out of her hypnotic state, looked across towards the house on the left. From the garden wall at home she could always see the red roof and she knew that Mrs. Halpin lived there. She often met her on the road from the town, weighed down with a bag of messages and a bucket of water and if anyone helped her to carry them as far as the cross, she'd give them sixpence. She always wore a black coat and a black beret. Miriam stared now with disjointed recognition at the woman in the uneven blue dress who, with white hair falling around her eyes as she scooped corn out of a saucepan and fingered it out to the hens pecking around her feet, called up to them on the line that ran above her paddock. "That's the way to make the money."

"That's how you have pucks of it, so," Shem shouted back.

"Is herself going to work too?" she laughed, and Monica, glancing back at Miriam, said, "We had to bring her to keep her quiet."

"I suppose your father is beyond in the field since daylight?"

"No, he has to work the first half-day but he'll be over after dinner."

"And that's not work at all, I suppose. He'd want to mind himself better than he does. I was looking at him there yesterday; he has himself killed going. Well, let ye go on, in the name of God, before the train comes."

6

Later on they left the railway, Shem going first and reaching down to haul them up the steep bank of scorched and withered grass. They leaned against the wire fence as the train passed; the engines now looked no different from the carriages since there was no longer a funnel spouting smoke that trailed behind it like a thick coil of grey hair on the wind and left a sulphurous smell over the fields. There was no longer a fireman who looked up and grinned at her out of the shiny blackness of his face as she leaned out through the bars of the railway gate and waved to the passing train. It was incomprehensible to her that things she had known from the beginning could change or disappear forever from the background of her life; she still thought every time that the next train would be the old one back again. Now people in the train lay back against the linen-covered head-rests, or read the papers, ate breakfast or looked out at the hills on the other side; one brown-skinned man, in pale grey clothes and with dark glasses, tilted his head to one side as he looked at them, fitting them into the morning landscape.

Crossing the fields she trailed behind them again. Ribs of wet grass stroked her ankles, wiping the dust off her brown leather sandals; the dew wet her feet, darkening the pale tan of her skin and the last strands of sleep unfolded from her mind. Underneath the high thick hedges the night still lurked where the low sun had not yet penetrated and she seemed to hear the sound of drops dripping off the twisting tendrils of the bushes onto the wet, shadowed grass. Her bare arms felt cold and she began to run and butted in between Monica and Shem and slipped her hands into theirs which were warm and dry and unaware of fear.

"You should have brought your cardigan," Monica said.

"She'll be roasted later on," Shem said and pointed out to them the low mist rising off the fields down towards the river, a sign, he added, that it was going to be a scorching day. But she still felt the chill creeping up the backs of her legs and she rubbed her knees together, high-stepping, lifting her feet above the reach of the prickling wet fingers of grass.

"For the love of God, will you walk on the ground like anyone," Monica asked, shaking off the hand that dragged out of her.

The gate onto the main road was locked with loops of wire so they climbed over it, and, crossing the road, turned down a lane narrower than their own. They came this way, the whole family, for a walk on Sundays, and after the glaring heat of the open spaces they'd wander gratefully into the scented shade of the lane, but now it seemed as shadowed and half-open as the rest of the world.

The beet-field too, when they reached it, appeared sunless and unfamiliar. In the middle of the headland the pony's cart rested on its shafts, and there they sat down to rig themselves out. Shem took a couple of sacks out of the cart and bandaged them one around each leg, tying strings of twine around them above and below each knee.

"Well, are you right yet?" he asked Monica who was still slithering and jerking into her wellingtons, her face red, her tongue clamped at the corner of her mouth with the effort. "Here's twine for you." He stood over her, directing her, showing her how to wrap the sacks and tie them, and when she stood up and they looked at the two thick tubes jutting down from her light green skirt, they fell around the field laughing.

"Well, now I'm equipped," she said, holding out one leg at a time as if she had silk stockings to admire, and she sniffed with satisfaction, conscious of a mature pride because for once, and without deliberation, she had laughed at herself as they were always telling her she should do. "Lead on," she said, giving Shem a push in the back.

Their father had hoed the first few drills after work the evening before so that the weeds were removed and the drills were pared down on each side and it was easy work to thin out the thick row of beet growing along the crest. Miriam followed them, skipping from one trench to another, sometimes behind them, beside them or walking

8

backwards before them, watching them as they kept pace with each other.

After a while she squatted beside a drill and began to tear away the extra plants, glancing across at the drills they had done to see what distance they had left between. She cleared a space up to a cluster of seedlings, then, reaching beyond them as Shem did, cleared away more at the other side, then returned her attention to the cluster. Carefully she tugged out the superfluous ones until there were only three close together, a strong one that should be left to grow and two frail ones which should be cleared away from it. Shem and Monica had finished a drill each. They turned at the headland and were heading back towards her. She groped among the stems, caught two and chucked them out. She looked with quick dismay at the frail one she had left to grow and which, deprived of the support of its neighbours and most of its own roots, slumped and limply lay down.

Shem looked up and seeing her stricken face he speeded up, passing out Monica. "Well, are you giving us a hand?" he asked, squatting on the far side of her scarred drill. He clasped his hands between his wide-apart knees and assessed the surviving seedling. "W——ell," he said, giving it the benefit of unheard extenuating factors. He reached out for her guilt-tightened fist and opened it and lifted out the squashed, once promising seedling. "Ah well," he said in brief requiem, then tossed it away, and reaching down to the weak one, he pressed its roots firmly into the earth and piled soil around it, clamping it close to the stem. "We might still get a little bag of sugar out of it," he said, sitting back on his heels and chuckling at her.

"What's she at?" Monica asked, almost flat out as she drew even with them. "I was just thinking," she said, wiping her forehead with her wrist, "if she's going to follow us around all day, she'll be dead; she ought to go and sit on the headland."

"The grass is a bit wet, yet. Come on," Shem said, taking her hand, "we'll fix up a place for you." He made a cushion of a pile of sacks in the cart and lifted her up into the front of it and threw his jacket around her shoulders. "Leave that on till the day gets warmer, and now don't move back too far or you know what'll happen."

Alone in the cart, she drew the corduroy jacket around her and stood up, moving this way and that to see herself. As she stepped back the cart tilted dangerously. She threw herself forward and crouched on the sacks and the cart lurched back into place and settled on its shafts. She looked fearfully at Shem but he hadn't seen her. It had happened at home one day, the cart had heeled up, its shafts shooting into the air and she had been thrown onto the ground and stunned. For days after that they wouldn't let her out of their sight and their protectiveness had disturbed her, suggesting danger even in familiar things.

She settled down now to watching them working towards her, their voices becoming more distinct; most times they'd call to her when they came to the headland and then they'd turn back on the next drill, and her heart would sink as they moved away again, their voices fading, the silence stealing back between them and her. And once they stopped on the far headland and for a moment she thought they were eating something but then she saw that it was cigarettes they had, and cherishing a feeling of unrecognised complicity, she stayed where she was.

The high bushes behind her were full of birds which chattered in a preoccupied way as they came and went all morning, bent on business. Then one small bird flew down to rest on the end of the cart. Lying still, she watched its bright gossipy eyes darting around yet not seeming to notice her until it saw her eyes blinking and then it stood still and watchful, and Miriam, remembering a picture in her mother's prayerbook, reached out a confident, inviting hand; but the affronted bird drew back its beak, then lifted itself and flew resentfully away to find a more private place.

At eleven o'clock they took a break. They spread Shem's jacket on the grass and Monica and Miriam sat on it. They opened the flask of tea and spread out the parcel of tomato sandwiches and fig-rolls and talked about all they had done already. But no more of the drills were hoed and now they had not only to thin the beet but also to pull away all the wild growth of weeds from the squat drills. In the increasing heat of the day the earth was dry and hard; the going was slow and after one drill Monica was exhausted. She had taken off the sacks and wellingtons and stretched her legs in the sunshine; now as their tea-break was nearly over she rested her tired back against the red wheel of the cart and picked and rubbed disconsolately at her stricken finger nails.

Shem, after a speculative glance at Miriam, lit a cigarette and when he had almost reached the end of it he stood up, ready for work again.

"I need another minute or two," Monica said.

When he had gone some distance she pushed herself further out into the sunshine and stretched out, rolling over on her front. "Oh, that's heavenly," she sighed, resting her head on her arms and turning her face to the sun. She encouraged Miriam to go off and gather daisies.

Later, when Shem was approaching along the next drill, she called Miriam back to her, unloaded her skirtful of daisies and showed her how to make a daisy chain, slitting a hole in the stem and linking the stem of another through it, and without raising her head she watched Shem as he turned at the headland and began another drill.

Next time he came back the Angelus was ringing, heard faintly from the town, and Monica was praying excessively with her head bowed in her hands. But she couldn't stay like that forever and when Shem came to the end of the drill he rested and said his prayers too. Then he hitched up his leggings before starting again.

"I suppose you're taking the rest of the day off," he said without expectation.

"I'll be with you in a minute," she snapped and tossed the chain into Miriam's lap. "I can't be everywhere at once." She began with distaste and without care to tie on the sacks again. Shem was already well down on the drill and working now at his own experienced pace so that she

11

had no hope of ever keeping up with him. And from then until dinnertime, as often as Miriam looked up, Monica was either standing, hitching up her ill-fitting leggings, or kneeling, one wrist rubbing her back and one her forehead as she gazed bleakly down the length of a drill at all that had yet to be done, and Shem passed by her, back and forth, working steadily, until at last he turned in on the end of her drill and worked towards her. She stood out of the way and let him finish the last few yards.

"Thanks," she said, dispiritedly, "I'm beat."

"Come on," he said, "it must be dinnertime, anyway." They gathered up their things and went home, where they were given the first of everything and treated as heroes.

* * *

For hours the sun had stood still, glistering with fierce heat so that she had to look away and when she looked again now it had begun to slip almost imperceptibly from its zenith. She leant against her father's knee; for the second time he had taken out his pocket watch and was rubbing it uneasily between his fingers before putting it back. It was nearly four o'clock, he said again, letting her see where the hands pointed. He was resting, propped against the high bank under the shade of the hedge and he still had the hoe gripped in one hand.

"They'll be bringing us the tea shortly," he said, looking across the field to the gate. Shem and the other man who had been there since dinnertime were working on nearby drills. "It'll be easier after this," he called across to them as they turned at the headland. "The worst of the heat'll be over."

Shem's bare, brown-red back glistened with olive oil and sweat. Monica was further away, moving heavily along by the drill, her progress hampered by the sack which she now wore as an apron tied around her waist. She had refused to tie them around her legs again when she found there was going to be a man in the field for the evening. Now each time she moved a knee forward it pinned down the sack, dragging it down so that she had to sit back on her heels again and again to hitch it up, and sometimes she looked as if she were going to lie down between the drills and never get up again, even though her father was going before her, hoeing them for her.

Miriam had gone with him, standing near him, absorbed in watching him. They were used to spending long hours together like that when he was gardening at home in the evenings after work. She followed him slowly, feeling the sun hot on her head. The tiny yellow flowers on her dress with their golden centres, seemed to spread and crowd together in the dazzling glare of the sun, blotting out the small white spaces between them. She stumbled sometimes on the roughness of the baked earth, seeing how it crumbled stubbornly and dusted her feet, blotting out the colour of her sandals. Her head was full of the sound of the wash of the river below the next field, and, near at hand, the rhythmic scuffing of the hoe and its occasional clinking against a stone or a buried chunk of broken glass. Sometimes she heard Shem and Murty talking and now and again they stopped to smoke, and after the first time Shem didn't bother to look to see if his father noticed. Murty's laugh was loud and rough and indifferent, and Shem had changed too; when she had gone over to them with the bag of sweets her father had bought for her, they smirked and took one each and when she saw that they had nothing to say to her, she walked away from them again.

Now, hearing a sound from her father and thinking he was going to say something to her, she looked up at him, squinting her eyes against the molten yellow sky. A large black bird sailed despairingly across the relentless face of the sun and drooped towards the shelter of the hedge, and she saw her father standing still, his hand clamping the handle of the hoe, his other hand clutching his chest and he loomed tall and dark as a shadow against the bright wailing sky and his face was dead white above the striped blue and white shirt and brown waistcoat and his hand on the brown cloth was white and lifeless.

13

After a vast lifeless moment he moved and slowly he took the hoe in both hands again and looked down at the drill, cautiously moving the hoe as if he might start working again. His breathing was guarded and then he remembered her and he looked unsmiling at her. He reached out and put his hand on her head. "That heat is too much for you. Come on," he said, "the pair of us'll go over and take a rest in the shade."

At four Ethna brought them their tea. She had made salad sandwiches, fresh, crusty rings of bread with lettuce, hard-boiled eggs, tomatoes and scallions and mayonnaise, and when she saw Murty, after the first bite, peeling back the corner of the bread, she turned on him and asked him if he didn't like them or what? For a minute he looked as if he were going to pretend he did, but when he saw Shem grinning he said that, to tell the truth he would have preferred a plain bit of bread and jam and Ethna told him that there was nothing wrong with him only that he didn't know the meaning of nutrition and did he know that it was bread and jam that had Irish people's teeth the way they were? Then with the pained dignity of a rejected missioner she turned her back on him, leaving him to the soothing influence of her father's conversation while she chatted with Monica, telling her about all the housework she had done, that she was going to do the shopping on the way home, and they discussed what they'd have for dinner the next day. Then she packed up, leaving another bag to Monica, and cycled away.

When she was gone, their father told Shem to start hoeing, and from where he sat he watched him, bristling with frustration. "Look here," he said, getting up and taking the hoe from him, "let you learn the right way, once and for all." When he had shown him how it should be done, he let Shem carry on while he got down on his knees and began thinning instead.

At seven they stopped working. Rubbing their hands down their sides, they looked out on their day's work.

"We're getting through it well," their father said. "Shem'll take the day off from school on Monday and that should see the end of it." Murty was rubbing his ear impatiently with his shoulder. "Aye, it should be a good crop, whoever'll live to see it. Well now . . ." He walked towards the gate with Murty. He was unrolling his own week's wages. Murty drew his wrist across his parched mouth, held out his hand for the money and loped away, flapping an indifferent hand to their father's courteous acknowledgement of his help.

Putting the rest of his money back in his pocket, he looked over the field again, taking no notice of their faces emptying of expectation.

"Well," he asked Miriam, "are you coming back with me on the bike, or what?"

"We'll keep her," Monica said, hitching up the bag Ethna had left her. "We're going down to the river to wash."

"Well be careful, now; don't go in too deep and don't stay out all night." Then he gave them a ten-shilling note each. "And you'll get it finished on Monday," he repeated to Shem, and Shem, his resentment all wafted away again, said he'd do it easily. "And sure we can't forget herself, she had a long day of it, too," he said and gave Miriam sixpence.

* * *

The grass grew high on the deserted bank of the river; the darkening ruins of a big house haunted the far bank; a tree grew at the water's edge and, holding on to its low straggling branches, they waded out into the water. Shem was sitting on the bank at a shallower part further down trying with the least immersion possible to wash himself. They had soap and a sponge and they scrubbed themselves and when the lather had floated away they splashed around, trying to swim, keeping one foot on the bottom. Their high clear voices splashed on the bare ruins of the old house and its lengthening shadows seeped across the rank grass towards them. They got out and dried themselves with rough towels that bore the compacted smells of soap-flakes, sunshine and fresh-air and hot ironing. They put on their clean clothes and wiped the grit out of their sandals, and towelled and combed their wet hair and rubbed cream on the sorest points of their sunburnt arms. And when the sun dipped at last behind the tips of the trees on the far bank they put on their cardigans, and when Shem rejoined them they went home, back across the fields and the railway, talking sometimes in tired exalted voices, the stillness of the evening marked by the cracking of the rails contracting as the heat of the day left them.

Sadness Is Over The Fields

IT WAS, after all her expectations, no different from any other night.

As she sat alone by the fire she turned dispirited eyes towards the silent television set glaring bleakly in the corner of the darkening kitchen and for a while she watched the soundless amazement of exclaiming Americans. She always wondered how people anywhere could have so many and such perfect teeth; she hadn't had one of her own left by the time she was thirty.

The News came on and she saw a car exploded in an empty street and then people crowded onto a pavement that was sprinkled with broken glass. She thought about her broken gate: she had remembered to close it: sometimes she forgot to and one night when she went out to close it the door had banged behind her and she had had to climb in through the window. But tonight she was more tired than usual and when she was tired she was always stiffer and even her will seemed to seize up so that she had to force herself to go on.

It had been a long day of unfulfilled waiting and now it trailed uselessly behind her. She still didn't know why her nephew and his wife hadn't come; she reached up to the mantelpiece for the postcard they had sent when they had arrived in Cork. It had a picture of a small house very like her own and set against a background of mountains; but in front of it, coming up almost to the door was the sea; that was the big difference and she looked thoughtfully at it for a long time. Then she re-read the message on the card and assured herself again that she had made no mistake about the date. She held it uselessly in her hands like a ticket for a raffle that was over and done with.

The weather forecast was on; she ignored the lines,

curves and arrows on the chart, but she thought by the
announcer's joyless face that he was predicting rain and
she turned away, unimpressed; through the back window
she could see the edge of the quiet sky still stained red by
the dying sun. It seemed to her that all communications
were unreliable.

She gave a listless sigh which at the last moment
gathered itself up and blossomed into an aching yawn that
dampened her eyes with weak tears and as she wiped them
away with the corner of her apron it occurred to her that
anyone might think she was crying; and seeing herself for
a moment through the eyes of a sentimental outsider she
felt sorry for herself. But it was a feeling she couldn't bear
to hold on to for long so she wiped her face, smoothed her
apron, put the card back on the mantelpiece and began to
prepare her supper.

She had been up early to have everything in order when
they arrived. She tidied and dusted until she was doing
more harm than good; she plucked critically at a corner of
the freshly washed curtains and when the hens, indifferent
to the neatly swept yard, came pecking around the door
the same as any other morning, she swept the new
tea-towel off the line above the fire and flapped it at them.
Dismayed at this abrupt chilling in a lifelong amiable
relationship, they turned and fled and she followed them to
the door. She'd rest her hand on the jamb and tilt her head
to listen but when no sound broke across the wide silence
of the fields she'd go back into the kitchen, stopping to
imagine how somebody new would see it.

When the sound of a tractor climbing the hill sent a
deep shudder through the noon-day stillness she hurried
out to meet Andy and to collect the messages he brought
from the town. She stood outside the gate, her hands
clasped under her apron as with nervous affability she
watched the quivering, belching tractor swerve in towards
her.

"Good morning, Andy," she called ineffectually
through the noise.

"Well, no sign of your visitors?" he asked as he jumped

18

down from the cab and walked around to the back of his unpainted trailer.

Gently she followed him along the grassy margin.

"No," she said as if she felt no anxiety, "not yet. Any news in the town?"

"Oh, not a stir," he said. He reached in among the churns he was bringing from the Creamery and drew out the big cardboard box, now more round than square from being packed with the messages he collected for the women on his route.

She saw a yellow car leave the main road at the foot of the hill. Quickly she took the parcels from Andy. He came to the gate with her.

"You may get that young fellow to fix it for you when he comes," he said, shaking it critically.

"Aye, well sure if he could..." she said undemandingly. It was a constant embarrassment to her; everybody who came in leaned on it, shook it or complained about it, but nobody offered to mend it.

She put away her groceries; she rolled the paper and the knotted broken twine into a ball and she was just stuffing it into the fuel box under the form when she heard the car coming up the hill. She re-tied the strings of her apron, tucked a strand of hair into her net while she looked around the kitchen for anything that might catch fire; and then, her heart pounding, she went to the door, holding back shyly into the shadows at the last moment.

The car passed slowly and a middle-aged woman with dark glasses and fat arms looked in and pointed at the bank of flowers against the front of the house; she glanced at the roof too. Years ago when there had been a thatched roof on the house people like that used to stop sometimes and ask her to allow them to take photographs. She never minded and sometimes she even let them persuade her to stand in too. Then one day somebody had spotted an old black shawl that had been discarded for years; the cats slept on it and that day it had been left out to air; they had suggested that she should put it around her shoulders and be photographed. Too embarrassed to resist she had just stood there while they draped her in it, plucking it this way and that, moving her from one place to another, telling her how to hold her arms and where to look and laughing all the time at their own inventiveness.

She had tried to suppress the shameful memory but sometimes even now it surfaced sickeningly. Back in the kitchen she looked with momentary misgiving at the picturesque house in the postcard.

By two o'clock she was feeling twinges of hunger. The hens too, not content to be put off forever, were coming back to the door in increasing numbers and at shorter intervals. At last she went out to feed them but first she put on her everyday overall and the boots she wore around the yard. She threw the hens their feed and hurried back inside to change again into her apron and shoes.

She made tea for herself; she cut a slice of bread, buttered it and brushed the crumbs off the table into her hand and threw them into the grate and put everything back into its place before she sat down to eat by the fire. As soon as she sat down she felt all the energy and interest that had carried her over the morning drain away, leaving her tired and apathetic, and she drank up the strong tea.

She was sorry now that she had let Andy go so soon; he was never in a hurry and most days he would stand around talking for as long as she encouraged him and it was through him that she kept in touch with the town. His call every morning was the high point of her days. Before she went to bed each night she'd go around the kitchen taking a note of what she wanted from the town so that she wouldn't delay Andy on his way to the Creamery. She would watch him go and the prospect of his sure return emptied the morning of its loneliness, suspending her for a while in the current of life. Sometimes, on his way home, if the day was cold or wet, he'd come in for a cup of tea, declaring that it would ruin his dinner, his figure and the strict diet his wife was keeping him on, but he'd drink it anyway and eat the currant buns she made.

When he was gone, the day would dwindle to its close.

Very rarely someone would call, maybe to visit her or to ask directions to some other house, but, though she was always glad to see anybody, the unexpectedness of a visit deprived her of all the pleasure of expectation and left her without any assurance of its recurrence but full of vague, unhappy awareness of spoilt opportunities. For though she craved company, she was shy with people and so agreeable that all the hard edges of her character, which had enabled her to survive without encouragement, were obliterated.

Left alone again, she was capable of forthright thoughts and talked to herself as she did her work or sat by the fire, reconstructing all the splintered and half-formed conversations she had had with her visitors.

On Sundays she went to Mass. All her life she had travelled on her bicycle but one morning she had fallen and afterwards the parish priest had asked for a volunteer, and a neighbour, who for years had passed her in frost and rain, had shame-facedly offered to give her a lift in his car. She accepted the ease it offered but it also meant that she had no time to stand around after Mass to talk with anyone she met.

On Fridays she would put on her coat and hat, put her black handbag into her shopping bag and walk down to the main road and wait for the bus to take her into the town to collect her pension. She would call at the shop to pay for the groceries Andy had brought her during the week. Then she'd buy a bag of jelly sweets and ten extra cigarettes and while she had two hours to wait for the bus she would go to visit her sister-in-law in the District Hospital.

She would climb the three flights of stairs to the wide gloomy landing that was hemmed in with dark wood-stained cupboards. On her third visit she had gone to the door of the ward and had looked in vain down the length of bright cheerful room for her sister-in-law. One of the patients had directed her to the other ward. She had crossed the landing and hesitated unhappily on the threshold.

Down either side of the ward which was painted a pale,

21

discouraging blue, there were eight beds. As she stood there one patient turned to look at her without optimism or expectation, darkened eyes looking out of a wrinkled face, glowing briefly with the spark of unexploited intelligence. The others were unaware of her.

She had found her sister-in-law asleep and would have gone away again but that the patient from the other ward, who was mainly responsible for the smooth running of the hospital, had followed her in and now masterfully shook her sister-in-law awake and while she was still dazed, turned her around in the bed, sat her up and propped a pillow behind her, warning her to stay awake now and to talk to her visitor and not have her wasting her time and her journey.

Her sister-in-law, when she had had time to sort out where she was and who had come to see her, accepted the bag of sweets, and holding them in her lap ate them in recurrent order, Strawberry, Greengage, Blackcurrant and Orange, dipping her fingers in for the next one while she sucked the first. Sometimes she remembered to offer her one.

A nurse came in.

"You're not giving her cigarettes, I hope?"

"I brought her a few."

"Well you may take them home again. Look at that!" She grasped the top of the bedclothes and peeled them apart, a sheet, two blankets and a bedspread. A dark brown-rimmed hole was repeated the whole way through. "She could have burned the place down only we saw her in time."

The obvious danger overwhelmed her careful mind and ever afterwards she would bring extra sweets instead of the cigarettes.

At home at night she would sit by the fire letting the heat soak into her knees before she went to bed, and she would say her prayers. But the formal rota of prayers and novenas would become inaccurate to her case as her mind bent under the weight of her single personal prayer of profound gratitude to God for leaving her her health.

Words would carry her no further. What she wanted was that her life should not deteriorate so that she ended her days in conscious ignominy, but she was afraid to mention it even in her own mind. God was good, she knew, and merciful and ultimately just, but He was also a law unto Himself and capable of sending you the most painful afflictions for your own eventual benefit.

It was evening when she awoke. The kitchen was dim; later on the setting sun would shine through the back window. Her head ached; her forehead had been tightened into a frown all the time she had slept and she felt a vague disillusionment which she couldn't account for. The kitchen had resumed its familiar appearance; it was still tidier and cleaner than on most days but it was no longer a stage set but the room she had shaped around her life. She still held the tea-cup in her lap; it had tilted over and there was a dark tea-stain on her new apron; and her shoes—she had polished them but already there was a light dusting of turf ashes on them that made them seem more her own.

Later, while it was still bright, she went out to close in the hens. She came to look at her flowers and to pull a few stray weeds from among them; she went to the gate and saw that the wire was looped through the latch. Before going in she stood to look around her. Everywhere was still as the sun slid away behind the hills. Away to the north she could see the pale blue blur of the Slieve Bloom mountains stretching away till their blueness was lost in the sky's. Long ago she had thought the blue was the sea and when her brother had gone away to England she had watched it for days, imagining she could see a ship on it, trying to imagine him away beyond that immeasurable distance. Later she had discovered that the sea couldn't be there; that what she saw was the outline of distant mountains. Much later when there was no longer an advantage in knowing precise facts, the childhood illusion had gradually reasserted itself until now she had almost forgotten that she had ever known the truth.

Separate Ways

"YOU'RE PACKING early enough, anyway," May said.

Beega jumped. Later on she wondered why she hadn't noticed the smell of peppermints in time.

"Well, it's easier to do it now than in the morning or when I come in tonight."

"If you left it too late you might have to stay here another day."

"There wouldn't be anything wrong with that," Beega said as convincingly as she could.

"No?" May enquired as she closed the door and wandered across to the window. Outside on the landing another door closed and they heard the preoccupied voices of guests going downstairs to dinner, parting on the stairs to let through a latecomer, exchanging greetings with the uncommitted familiarity of people who've seen each other at meals every day for a week, or at times with the over-reaching friendliness of someone who wanted every acquaintance to be significant and unforgettable.

"Of course not. Anyway you're going to need the room. Leo says you're booked out for the rest of the month."

"And Leo is the one who knows." She slung sulkily across the room, her exercise sandals slapping her heels.

Beega knelt down to lock the suitcase on the floor. She fumbled with the key. "I don't think it's good for you to wear those sandals while you're expecting," she said, because of all the things she had been itching to say and hoped she could refrain from saying in the short time they were together, that seemed to have the least potential for damage.

"Anything else I'm doing wrong?" May snapped as if she had waited for days, sensing everything that Beega noted and disapproved of, deliberately not correcting anything until Beega would be goaded to a pitch of irritation she couldn't control. Then she'd abandon the awful spinsterish deference she seemed to feel she owed her since May's precipitate marriage had disrupted the co-ordinated progress of their lives. Beega looked at her defiant, waiting face and saw all the familiar signs she hadn't known she remembered. She had begun to hum unconvincingly under her breath and tried to stop it when she recalled that years ago May had asked her if that was her ladylike way of whistling in the dark. Briskly she swept the rest of her clothes one by one off the chair, folded them and stacked them in the open case on the bed. But she was still humming.

May fingered the clothes in the case beside her and unfolded with one hand a pair of hipster slacks. "Well for you, you can wear clothes like that," she said and cast them aside.

"You never liked them anyway," Beega said, retrieving them and packing them again. She locked the case and swung it onto the floor beside the other.

May dipped again into her pocketful of peppermints. "Have one?"

"I've just brushed my teeth." She opened her bag and pushed back the curtain for light to see her make-up. "What are you doing for the rest of the night?" She asked at random because she couldn't bear to have them both concentrating solely on her face. When there was no answer, she held the mirror aside and glanced at May. "Hm?"

With glacial malice May stared at her, her eyebrows lifted, begging her to suggest, honestly, just what she might find to do in such a place. She mooned around the house most of the day in her nightdress, with her long dressing gown open and floating behind her as she plied dreamily between the box of peppermints on the sideboard, a magazine on a table, a bowl of flowers on the windowsill, the mirror over the mantelpiece. Mostly the guests were out of the house all day fishing, or sometimes Leo led a party of them up into the mountains, and when they were near the end of their stay they would go out sight-seeing and shopping. They went to bed at nine or ten o'clock every night just when May thought the day should be starting, and in the mornings they were up again at six, hours before May would even consider sitting up in bed to eat the breakfast which one of the girls would bring up to her from the kitchen. Eventually she would get up and wander downstairs where there was still nothing for her to do that wasn't already being done adequately since long before she had ever come there.

Sometimes if she saw a new duster in use she would take it and go around flicking it over the backs of chairs, a task she immediately felt disinclined to continue; she'd peel back the edge of a handkerchief or scarf bundled in a corner and find it full of odd shaped and coloured stones or shells; she'd open a tin on the hall-stand and touch with dismal uninterest the peacock colourful flies; as she skirted a corner she'd remember to pluck aside the hem of her dressing gown, but there was nothing there to distress her anymore: the cans of live bait which in her early and brief enthusiasm as chatelaine she had upset, and which had spilled on the floor while she stood screeching as they squirmed and wriggled at her feet had, with all the rods and reels, been banned for her safety and peace of mind to an outhouse. But with their equipment had gone all the company. In the evenings after dinner they used to sit around the fire with Leo for an hour or two until bedtime, at ease in the uncomplicated ambience of bachelorhood, talking of the way they had passed the day. Now in May's burgeoning presence they felt vaguely ashamed of their celibate obsessions and sat outside on the steps or went to their own rooms and wrote to their wives.

"Where are you going now?" she asked Beega, as if her sister's plans were bound to exclude her.

"Into the town. I have to ring Tom, let him know what time I'll be back tomorrow."

"Doesn't he know that?" May said, looking as all married women eventually did when they came to realise that such considerate attentions were a poor investment. But neither did she wish to encourage Beega to retain her sovereign independence now that she had lost her own. "Anyway, you could ring from downstairs."

"I'd rather ring from the town."

"More private?"

"Yes," Beega said emphatically, implying that it was an observance that might with benefit be more widespread.

"Ooooh," May said, "touchy."

"Get your coat and we'll go."

"I'm not going."

"But why? Ah, come on, it's my last night."

"But not mine, is it."

They stared at each other. May felt she had a lot of ground to make up. She had been elaborately and imaginatively hospitable at first – she had been so glad to see Beega again – and had set out wholeheartedly to enjoy the time she was there. It was near the end, when she realised that Beega had only a few days left and was already packing away clothes she wouldn't be wearing again, that she saw her mistake. She had shown Beega a lifestyle of leisure and comfort and optional activity, of picturesque health and freedom in the open air, and for nights the vivid life of a tourist centre twenty miles away. It was just the kind of impression that would appeal to Beega and send her home with fulsome ideas of May's contentment. And to crown it all she seemed to regard Leo with a kind of reverent fascination.

"If you'd drive the car you could go when and where you liked."

But May refused to drive as if any show of self-reliance might weaken her plea of intolerable privation.

"I've had enough driving for today," she said. And because she knew that her grievances and excuses didn't stand up to unsympathetic examination, she added, unarguably, "I'm tired."

When Beega returned, hours after, the house was in

darkness save for a glimmer of light in the front room, and as she crossed the gravel the drone and murmur of the men's voices came to her through the open windows. A chair scraped across the floor as it was pushed back. Somebody was going to bed. She heard the sudden effort of the torpid voices bidding him goodnight and she waited outside so as not to prolong the leavetaking.

They were sprawled in the chairs, stupefied with tiredness after the exertions of the day in the open air, dinner in the evening and afterwards the illicit whiskey to which Leo alone reacted positively. Through the open doorway he saw her as she crossed the hallway to the stairs.

"Come on in," he called, holding out his hand which nevertheless fell limply down by the chair while he waited for her. The idea charmed her but she had already heard the resentful plodding of May's feet across the landing from the bathroom. Still she went to the door to see who was with him. Two of the men stood up then and shyly said goodnight as they passed by her and went upstairs. Only Paul, a Frenchman who came every year and was on easier terms with the family – which, she was startled to realise, included her – stayed on.

"Well, where did you go this evening?" Leo enquired, the way her mother's friends years ago might have asked: What did you learn in school today? Though not quite the same, she recognised, as she rubbed her aching neck inside her upturned collar and leaned against the jamb of the door. She stared with wonder and weariness into the shadowy room. She was conscious too of the visitors asleep upstairs, a dozen or more of them restoring their healthy minds and the healthy bodies to accommodate them. Leo was drowsy but ready to stir himself if she had anything to tell him. He was watching her and she gave him a reluctant, resentful halfsmile. When he was like that, being sociable and friendly and with an uncertain particle of a smile frozen on his lips as if he were going through a routine he had been taught and didn't believe in, it was almost as if he wished indeed that he could feel the kind of interest people often had in the minutiae of each other's lives.

She told him the hotel she had been in. She was faintly embarrassed; it seemed to her that he hardly approved of her mixing two kinds of holiday, and he was intrigued to know why she couldn't take the country as it was without resorting to the popular tourist zone of souvenirs and postcards and bland hotels. She had spent the evening in one, sitting alone in the corner of the lounge, her finger freezing on the rim of a glass, monitoring her own sobriety as she cushioned each glass of vodka on a glass of pineapple.

"I'd better go up and see May," she said.

"I suppose it's near time we all went," he said. "What time is it?" With considerable, yet not enough effort he arched his neck to see the clock on the wall above his chair.

"It's gone twelve."

"Gone twelve," he murmured as he gazed in wonder into the fire. He crouched forward, holding the glass in his hands between his knees, and slowly shook his head. Some mystery that had always puzzled him had begun to haunt him again lately, and he was no more married now nor less solitary than he had been over a year ago when they had first met him, and she knew now how little she would have injured him by making the very suggestion that had been forcing itself on her and she had been fanatically avoiding — that May should return home. Even when he had been seeing May twice and three times a day in the short time he had known her, he had no real conviction that, even if she did marry him, she would ever stay with him. And now, in so far as he cared at all about other people's opinion, he felt a vague hangover of embarrassment for the inappropriateness of it all: that after a term, the duration of which he had no way of knowing, but which May was already allotting with haphazard instinct, she would leave him.

"I've never seen anything like it," the forgotten and forgetful Frenchman was musing wistfully, and it was the foreign tinge of his accent that made Beega look at him with mothering, dolorous eyes.

"Aye," Leo said, "if he had been ready for it . . ." and his voice sighed away into the silence of the night.

The room was dimly lit with two electric candles above the mantelpiece and the wavering flames of the fire; and shadows swirled and loomed and toppled on the walls around them. Two pairs of canvas shoes were drying on the hearth; the dog was asleep behind a chair and sometimes when he was disturbed he thumped his tail against the door of the dresser behind him.

"Won't you have some?" Leo said eventually, waving towards the bottle.

Without considering the reasons she had always had for declining, she took up a glass off the tray and walked across the room, picking her steps over the Frenchman's feet – later, with bleary recollection of courteousness, he drew them back. She poured half a glassful from the unlabelled bottle and resting on the arm of a chair, she too stared at some random focus. In the flickering smoky dimness they listened to the sedgy silence of the night outside on the wasteland that spread out to where the sea crept up on it, insinuating itself into the weak points, making inroads, isolating small islets that were demolished until nothing was left but a jag of rock and sometimes in a crevice a clump of rough grass that craved landward in the wind when the tide was low.

She yawned deeply, trying not to open her mouth, and in anguish she pressed her face into her hand and said, Oh, Lord, and slowly swung her head to loosen the tiredness of her neck and shoulders. She clutched the glass and drank. Her head soared gently, split open and the stars showered down into the swarming well of her mind. She held her breath and bit by bit the parts of her head reassembled and everything – and eventually the roof of her mouth too – slid back into place.

The dog was thirteen years old. She sat into the chair and peered down over the side of it at him. He couldn't live

30

much longer, though one wet night last summer, on their first visit, when they were all sitting around the room, a German vet had caught the dog's head and looked at its eyes and teeth and then turned him over on his back on the floor, embarrassing them all with his further examination before saying he had seen one live for eighteen years. It was a great age – for a dog – everyone wanted to comment and was lost when somebody else said it first, because then there was nothing else they could think of to say. They just had to stare at the dog with the homage that was expected for him, and try to look impressed and full of thought about the relativity of age between man and animal, until the dog himself padded blindly away between the chairs and released them.

Somewhere and sometime in the night, Leo said, "Will I top that up for you?" and because she was yawning again she put her hand over the glass. The Frenchman had put down his glass and his head was almost touching the floor as he bent forward in his chair and looked back under it for his shoes. He wore grey socks, and as she stared at them, though her eyes were streaming, she felt as disappointed as if she had met the Shah of Persia in a peaked cap. Before he went up to bed he said goodnight in a stiff formal way that always left her puzzled for a while, he was so friendly all the rest of the day.

"I suppose I'd better go too," she said, though it might have been an hour later.

"He's a fine chap, Paul," Leo said in the tired droning voice that reminded her sometimes of bees in an orchard and then again of an Anglo-Irish clergyman's funeral voice saying: "Thy will be done."

"He comes back every year," he added, as if such friendship sustained him but left him unconsoled.

One last half-solid piece of coal was poised on a pile of clinker that dimmed gradually and cracked; Leo touched it in time with the side of his shoe and knocked it back into the diminished heart of the fire where the last flames swarmed around to consume it and when she noticed it again it was reduced to a cinder and the whole fire was dead except for the distant winking of a spark here and there.

"I got iron tablets for May in the chemist's," she said once when she had counted the ticking of the clock to eighty-nine and she heard the two semi-circular plinks of the bottle as he left it on the table. "Good," he said, and after a while he asked, "Do you think she needs them?" And later on she said, "They won't do her any harm, anyway." And still later he agreed, "No, that's true." And so their minds drifted, touching at one point of conversation, then diverging in separate paths but circling back eventually to the one tangential point.

May was asleep, lying back against three pillows. Beega left the tablets on the dressing table and began listlessly from habit to rearrange the bottles and jars and jewellery that were jumbled there and the clothes scattered on an armchair and spilling onto the floor; but there were odds and ends belonging to Leo among them and she shied away from them, switched May's slippers into a marginally tidier position before leaving the room. Downstairs Leo was in the kitchen, packing lunches for the next day.

"If you'd let May do all that," she had said, "she mightn't have so much time to be discontented."

"I don't think she'd want to," he said, and she was relieved and reproved when he left it at that.

Though she would grow used to him and learn to perceive and understand him beyond all the careless assumptions of familiarity, there would always be an echo of wonder at the way he re-emerged to carry on the routine of his days, since effort hardly seemed possible without optimism.

An Old Story

ON SUNDAY the man was there as usual, fishing on the stretch of river below their house. That, Delia's grandmother said, was a good sign. She was anxious to interview him. Delia, for all the Sundays she had spent out there with him, could give no consistent, satisfactory answers to her repeated questions: Who was he? Where did he come from? What did he work at? And could she swear to it that he wasn't married already?

Meanwhile, Delia's mother leaned against the jamb of the door and looked out at the road.

"Does he know the state you're in?" her grandmother asked Delia, and Noreen turned her head and glanced with a brief glimmer of curiosity at her daughter. But she had heard it all before and when she saw a new car coming over the bridge she cut across her own mother's words. "It's early days yet," she said and called Delia to come over, quick, to the door.

"Why, what's happening?" When eventually Delia strolled across to peer out over her mother's shoulder, the car had sped past.

"You're too late. You could have got a lift if you'd been out there."

"But I'm not going anywhere. Who was it, anyway?"

"Who do you think? How many do you know that has a car like that?"

"One of the Galvins?" Delia guessed, recalling a streak of shining red past the door.

"One of the Galvins," Noreen mimicked. "Six marks for Delia." But her daughter had outgrown her and it still confused them both. "Go back in and sit down," she snapped. It had always been her delight to tease Delia

33

every time T. J. Galvin passed the house, which he had to do countless times in a week since most of their farm was on the other side of the river. "Now we know who has his eye on Delia," she'd say. Later on, when Delia was beginning to grow up, she'd look her over sometimes to see if there was anything she might do to improve her appearance. But it was as much as she could do to maintain her own. Besides, she felt that while Delia had youth on her side she'd get by. And then there was no money, ever, for anything, let alone gilding the lily. "Take that old string off your hair, why don't you," was the most she could suggest if she happened to be there when Teresa Barry would call for Delia to go out. Then Noreen would take up her position at the door and watch them walking down the road and impartially compare their attributes, until they were out of sight or somebody else stopped to talk to her.

Meanwhile the two girls would walk on, often as far as the main road, until someone would give them a lift to a match, to a carnival, or anywhere.

They had had enough of school, both of them, but later in the summer when they were bored with the long days of trailing up and down the road, waiting for something to happen – though it never did and they had no money to take them where it might – they thought it would be a great idea to go to Dublin and get jobs there.

The house Teresa worked in was attached to a Bar, the company was adult, varied and receptive, and there Teresa settled in and prospered. Delia, on the other hand, found herself confined to a house with eight children whose mother immediately took advantage of her presence to go out more, as everybody had recommended, to alleviate the stress and isolation which had been getting her down. Too much of it soon began to impress itself unpleasantly on Delia too, and when she went home for her one-Sunday-off-in-the-month she neglected to go back.

Her grandmother – the one person from whom she might have expected a warm welcome – showed no pleasure at having Delia returned to her. She had been greatly upset when Delia had left home – Delia, whom she had trained from her earliest days to minister to her needs, needs her own daughter was too preoccupied to take note of. Many a night Noreen had gone out, nobody knew nor enquired where, with one man or another, and the old woman, no longer able for the journey to the village, was left alone. This was before Noreen's adventures had yet borne Delia who in time would become her companion and messenger. Then when Noreen went out at night and the two subsequent children were in bed, Delia would set out for the village with her grandmother's money in her handkerchief. She'd bring her home a Baby Power and for herself a bottle of lemonade or sweets or a comic with which they would soothe the long night. At eleven o'clock they would help each other to bed; Delia would unlace her grandmother's shoes and the old woman would comb Delia's long, tangled black hair before they climbed into their bed. Delia had spent more time with her than ever Noreen had, and she was finally attuned to her grandmother's tastes in the line of conversation, refreshment and privacy.

When Delia was sixteen, her devotion lessened. She became erratic and half-hearted in her attentions and her grandmother knew that Delia would soon be gone and she would be left once more to Noreen's wayward mercies.

In the short time Delia spent in Dublin, her younger sister, Bernie, had taken her place as companion to their grandmother, who, having learnt her lesson, had now also enlisted their half-brother Tim, and was training him to run messages for her too. Now she saw no advantage in Delia's return, nothing but the danger that she would infect Bernie with her own dissatisfaction.

And so her days since coming home were spent as before, walking up and down the roads, but alone now, talking with anybody who'd stop, or rambling into other houses. All her life she had been susceptible to the appeal of the orderly lives of their neighbours. It seemed to her an unsurpassable arrangement whereby a woman would stay at home and have as many sons and daughters as she liked but all of the same identifiable father who spent the day earning money for them, came home to them every night and took them for a drive on Sunday.

So enamoured was she of the regular-breathing, smooth-running atmosphere of their houses, that when one or another of these women asked her if, now that she had come back and might be happier in a job near home, she might like to work for them, she always said yes. And she would begin, dreamily, the following morning. But it was one thing to wander in as an idle neighbour at eleven o'clock in the morning; to have sandwiches and Bovril made up for her by a contented, pitying woman who thought poor Delia was half-starved; to be given an old dress or a jumper or a pair of shoes which might fit her; or even just to sit in the corner beside the range while the woman ironed clothes at the table and in clinical detachment probed Delia with long-handled, curving, spiked questions nobody else would have answered. It was altogether different to be engaged to work for one of them; to be treated no longer with inquisitive tolerance as a returned traveller with tales to tell, a naive, exploitable entertainer whose unpredictable visits served to break the monotony of housebound days, but instead to be ordered to do this, do that and don't waste time chattering. Discussions were frozen when she came into a room, and if there were visitors she was always given something to do that kept her in the back-kitchen or the outhouses. And so gradually she accumulated the impression that she was being watched over and her movements restricted, and though she didn't examine this condition nor enquire the reasons behind it, she dimly registered a feeling of incompleteness, of not being allowed to enter into the fullness of their family life as she had longed abjectly to do. But while her enchantment with these women, once she began to work for them, was short-lived, her desire to emulate their life-style increased painfully.

She stayed longer with Mrs. Galvin than with anybody else. The Galvins' daughter, Joan, was getting married at that time and the novelty of the wedding preparations so absorbed Delia that for a while the usual pattern of eagerness, decay of interest and then defiant carelessness until she left or was told to go, was deflected and she stayed on. But not to the satisfaction of her employers. For, being willing to spend unstinted hours looking after the wedding clothes, when her offers to bring them down and press them were declined she would steal upstairs and, standing before the long mirror, she'd hold the white dress up to herself. Meanwhile, all the rough, routine work of the house and yard she left to the Galvins. In this situation they writhed for a week or two, eager to get Delia out of their hair, yet cherishing the idea of having a servant at hand for the weeks ahead when there would be a constant stream of visitors to the house to be entertained and impressed. In the end, hard-edged realism won over fanciful notions and on Saturday night Mrs Galvin gave Delia an extra week's wages and told her that from now on she would manage the housework on her own.

And so the following morning found Delia trailing home from Mass at her old unencouraged pace, alone again, hands in pockets. Stopping on the bridge, she heaved herself onto the parapet, one of the solitary diversions she used to enjoy and sought now to recapture. Instead she saw the fisherman on the bank of the river where he had often been before. Teresa and she used to take it in turns to sit on his scooter which was parked in the gateway, pretending to drive it. "If we don't get a lift," Teresa would say, "we'll go down and talk to him." But it had hardly ever come to that. Now all the cars had gone from the road after Mass and the Church-going world was pouring milk over cornflakes and shaking the Sunday papers into position. The monotonous wash of the river over the silence of the morning was studded by the tapping of a shoe against the stone bridge.

It was dark inside their own kitchen and smelled always of smoke. The windows were too stiff ever to be opened and it was aired only whenever the day was mild and her grandmother agreed to have the door left open. Bernie was sitting on the edge of the table, dangling her feet in a pair of sandals with a frayed strap which one of the Galvins had given Delia.

"Take them off this minute, you little brat."

"Keep your hair on," Bernie said. "Who says they're yours?"

"She gave them to me."

"Well, she won't be giving you any more, will she?"

But the loss of a job was not an emotive issue in their house and could not be used with any conviction to needle her. Their grandmother was sitting in her usual place by the fire, toasting bread on a fork. She didn't intervene, which Bernie regarded as a victory for her, while to Delia it was yet one more indication that she had lost forever her favoured place. She poured herself a cup of tea and loaded it with sugar and milk. She buttered a slice of bread and sprinkled sugar on that; then stood at the door to eat her breakfast. After the amenities of Mrs. Galvin's kitchen, she no longer felt inclined to do anything at home, so now when she had finished she left her cup on the window sill and went out.

"How do stand it?" Delia complained, "doing nothing all day Sunday only fishing."

"How do *you* stand it?" he replied "doing nothing at all any day of the week."

After his lunch, which he shared with her, he picked up his rod and satchel and they wandered downstream under the outer eye of the bridge where the water was shallow.

She balanced on a flat stone and, tilting back her head, looked up at the stone bridge arching above them where they stood side by side.

"It's like a chapel," she said, her voice filling the space around them.

He looked at her.

"Come on," he said, moving along; and since she had her hand on his shoulder for balance she had to go too.

"Won't they be wondering about you at home," he asked when they emerged on the far side of the bridge, "where you are, out all the time?"

38

"They might, all right," she said the first time, looking back towards home, and then looking at his face. "Maybe I'd better go." And she did, slipping off her shoes and splashing away through the water. But she came out again the following Sunday to meet him, and he was there, the scooter parked in the same place. And this time when he said "Shouldn't you be getting on home?" she shrugged her shoulders.

"Does your mother not ask where you go?"

"Ah, my mother . . ." she said hopelessly.

"Leastways, she managed things better than you did in your day," Delia's grandmother said to Noreen when it transpired that the fisherman was quite willing – without passionate enthusiasm, maybe, but nonetheless willing – to marry Delia in good time and to take her back to his own side of the country.

"Hah!" Noreen scoffed. "Giving up her freedom and going off to live among strangers and be a servant to them all her days. Do you call that managing? I managed as well as I wanted to manage, thank you very much."

"You're the one to talk about strangers! Every bucko from hell to Bethlehem slouching up to the door in the dark winter nights. Or whistling behind the hedge for you to come out. And your ladyship, of course . . . hah!" The old woman lifted her hands, held them fatalistically in the air, then brought them back to rest again. "Hah!" she repeated, as if her daughter's behaviour might have been predicted from the beginning of time. "Out with her on the minute, no questions asked, go a bit of the road with everyone. And then as soon as the bright evenings were in and they saw the shape you were taking, away with them over the hills. Off to re-join the regiment, moryah. And it's farewell to thee, my bonny wee lass."

"Take care," she called after Noreen, "that it's not one of her own the child'd be marrying." She would say his name several times a day, suddenly, unexpectedly springing it on Noreen, to see if it would jog her memory. But Noreen had shown no sign of recognition, or distress, even in the beginning before she had spotted her mother's ploy. Now she would laugh and walk away without answering.

Nevertheless they set out to make a big occasion of Delia's wedding. Among their neighbours too, Delia's emergency provoked a great flourish of philanthropy and a fulsome wish to see her married with the least possible ignominy. She had a choice of three wedding dresses, a selection of hats and veils to choose from; discreet presents of new underwear and one of second hand stuff; and where imagination faltered they gave her cash. Mrs. Galvin, having the recipe to hand, made the wedding cake. "Delia, weren't you a terrible girl," she said as she weighed the flour, "to go and get yourself in that state at this hour of your life."

"But he'd never have thought of getting married if he didn't have to," she said and bit a glacé cherry.

The wedding was all they had expected of it. Delia, moved by their generosity, had gone around on the previous Sunday inviting them all to the reception, a reversal of hospitality which set them off balance for a while until they unshouldered their dignity and decided they could make a great day of it. "Delia girl," they'd say, "we're going to miss seeing you on the road," or "We'll be lonesome not having you to call in on us anymore." Their heavy sincerity was leavened by the memory of all the times they had said that something should be done about her, not to have her streeling along the roads at all hours.

The honeymoon was to be spent in Dublin, after which Delia and her husband would return to live with his mother. With her bridegroom Delia left the reception in a shower of confetti, a dress which wouldn't fit her for much longer, and a borrowed car. The neighbours went back into the bar for another drink and tipsy wives nudged reeling husbands to offer Noreen a lift home afterwards. But with the last of her gift money Delia had hired a car for her mother for the day and Noreen rode away in style in her own time.

On her first Sunday morning in her new home, Delia woke to the sound of activity in the kitchen. Her husband was there, packing a box of sandwiches. She blinked at him in the dimness – this kitchen was darker than their own had been.

"There's tea in the pot, there," he said when he saw her. "You could take my mother a cup in the bed and I'll be getting on."

"Why, where are you going?"

"I'm going fishing," he began to say, and then he stopped to look at her as he fixed the rod to the scooter which was parked in the porch. "Now where," he asked patiently, "did you think I'd be going on a Sunday?"

You Wouldn't Throw
Me To The Lions, Would You?

THE DOCTOR hovered in the kitchen doorway, blinking in the fluorescent lighting that blinded him after the dim, economy bulbs of the bedroom, stairs and hall and he kept tapping his knee with his black bag, jutting out the knee to meet it each time as if he were about to genuflect. Otherwise he looked sleepy, amiable and forgetful.

"Well, that's that," he said, with a tone of mournful finality but seeing Mary-Jo's puncturing glance he giggled and scratched his tousled head.

Abruptly she returned her attention to the five beakers of coffee she was making and he, recollecting that she might still be emotionally involved, cleared his throat and reached up to straighten his tie but there was no tie, only the rumpled collar of his red and green striped pyjamas over which he had dragged on his clothes.

She filled up two of the beakers and offered him one. Relieved, he came into the kitchen for it.

"Well," she said dismally, "did he urgently need your attention?"

He stroked and rubbed his wide nose with sterilised fingers and shook his head.

"Nothing a discreet and kind-hearted wife couldn't have tended to." His voice became more analytical. "You see 'em at it in the Westerns: just up with the skirt and tear a scelp off the petticoat and wrap it around the bullet wounds." He sniffed aridly. "Can I have a drop of milk in this? You'll ruin your nerves, girl, on black coffee." He was fiddling with the air extractor over the cooker. "I suppose that's why you never get a whiff of food around this place?"

"One of the reasons," she said, hesitating over the half

bottle of milk which was all she could find. She slammed the door of the vast fridge and two tins of sardines rattled obsequiously in the rack.

As they drank their coffee in silence, they looked around the modern, minutely equipped kitchen. They could hear on the floor above them the relentless footsteps of Marian and Julia, one on either side of Mel's bed.

"Will you remind me to tip off Marian not to pull the bedclothes too tight around him," he said, betraying his line of thought too. "Until we see what damage there is to his leg," he added.

Mary-Jo nodded indifferently; she held the cup in both hands away from her mouth and her eyes were wide with joyless reflection.

* * *

"I could have sworn that was Mel I heard in the lounge," Julia had said again. She went on shovelling dessert into her mouth with an expression of busy curiosity as if she still had hopes of finding something new and wonderful in the next mouthful. Nothing happened. The spoon rattled in the empty plate. "Really, it's not worth the money," she said, settling her arms on the table and shelving her rustling, tricel-covered bosom on them. She sealed her lips against a self-induced belch and un-inhibitedly looked around at the people at the other tables.

Mary-Jo, eating her own dessert without expectation, lowered her calm eyes. Boredom ballooned in her mind, squeezing out every other passing sensation.

The waitress brought them tea and collected Julia's plate; she reached for Mary-Jo's but Julia shook her head and the impressionable girl left them.

"Eat it up, girl," Julia said and reached across with her teaspoon and encouragingly did it for her. "You won't get back your money because you're too finicky to eat what they give you," she continued as if expounding a whole philosophy for life. "Now drink your tea and we'll go look for Mel."

"Julia, it's late. By the time we're home and unpacked . . ."

"They won't be waiting up for you at home, will they?"

"N-no," she said, thinking of her tranquil father scurrying up to bed at the prospect of a midnight visit from Julia.

"Well then! And I'll drive, so come on!"

With their handbags on their arms they strolled down the broad silent corridor. They stopped to glance through the first glass door. Inside it was dark save for the blue flicker of a television set in front of which sat gentle, disappointed men who had expected to be doing something quite different by now. With them women in sleeveless dresses, pastel-coloured cardigans over their shoulders for the evening, and fragile shells of blue hair, women who thought in the weakness of relief that it was well to be so well.

"We won't find him there," Julia said, moving on. "What's that he used to say about letting it live our lives for us?"

Julia's careless attempts at quoting people always got under her skin. She paused to look again, to see how in ten or twenty years' time she could hope to spend her holidays.

"Isn't it less likely that we'll find him here?" she asked as she followed Julia into the bar. She held the door as it glided and closed behind her. She was the first to see Mel and she knew even as she prayed how hopeless it was to pray that Julia would turn away now.

"Mel!" Julia was exclaiming as she loomed above his table in a dim corner.

"Zhulia?" He shook his light head to erase the image tossed up by his troubled imagination. As the illusion hardened into reality, a look of infinite sadness attenuated his features and he held up a gentle but unswervable hand. "No! I'm not coming with you."

"I'm not going home myself, yet," Julia said happily and turned to wave Mary-Jo forward to the sport. "Come on. Isn't this great!" But her eyes glinted, the first sliver of impatience with Mary-Jo's demurs showing through now that after a fortnight abroad when they had been dependent on each other for moral support, they were at last within reach of home and had met the first person they knew.

"And Merry-Jo came too," Mel said with the dawning sad wisdom of Caesar when he saw who had put the knife in his back.

Julia bounced on the cushioned chair, thrilled that there was another kick left in her holiday, one the travel agent hadn't promised.

"Imagine meeting you here! What are you doing so far from home? Is Marian with you? And the kids, are they well?" She scattered questions over him as she opened her bag and rooted for her purse.

Meanwhile Mary-Jo sat down. "Hello, Mel," she said gently and then her eyes fixed on a point above and beyond Julia's money-counting fingers.

Julia left them and went to the bar.

"That stupid barman," she said as she sat down again, washing heedlessly over the silence between them. "Was Mary-Jo telling you about the great time we had in Spain?"

He raised his eyebrows, then nodded as recollection illuminated his hazy mind.

"Yeah, she was here writing it with her finger on the table. So that's where you're coming from. I had an idea I hadn't seen you around the place this while back."

"Well, honestly," Julia pouted, tucking in her shoulder as the barman placed their drinks on the table. "We sent you a postcard; I don't know but that we sent you two and that's all the heed you put in it. We'll know better the next time. Now," she hissed as the barman withdrew, "back to what I was going to say. He nearly refused, didn't want to serve another drink for you; he said you'd had enough. I told him not to be an ass, you got drunk once when you were sixteen and you were a pioneer since and anyway the lemonade was for you." But she took the empty glass out of his hand and sniffed. "Mel! What came over you? Where's your pin?" She turned over the lapel of his coat. "God," she said and laughed but she was shocked. Mary-Jo looked on with a patient endurance that appalled herself.

"Little boys get tired of lemonade," he said and his voice was sour and weary. He looked to Mary-Jo for insight and noted her glass of vodka. "I see you have a working respect for anaesthesia, too. Do you remember the time you were here before?"

"Was I?"

"We were."

"Did Marian change the carpet in the lounge yet?" Julia butted in briskly.

"What? Oh, you can pick it with her. I leave all that to Marian. I'm leaving all that to Marian," he corrected himself introspectively.

Time passed unsatisfactorily. Julia's enthusiasm for Mel's company curdled as he became quieter and drunker. It seemed unlikely to Mary-Jo that Mel had ever acquired any taste for company for its own sake; years ago when he had been sober and self-contained, his preference for solitude had suggested some kind of philosophy that set him apart from everyone else she knew.

"We'll be back in a minute," Julia warned him as she stood up, gripped her bag and jerked her head at Mary-Jo who tamely followed her from the room.

In the powder-room, Julia looked over her circumspect shoulder, then rounded on Mary-Jo.

"Well, what are you going to do about him?"

"Me? About Mel? What can anyone do?"

"That's what I'm asking you. After all, he's your responsibility."

"Mine?"

"Well, more than mine, anyway. You're supposed to be his friend."

"So are you."

"It's not the same – you were nearly married to him, don't forget."

"Don't let me, will you."

"Well, anyway you can't let him get into a car and drive home — that journey and the state he's in! You'd have it on your conscience for the rest of your days. Imagine facing Marian if anything happened to him and to have to admit we met him here and saw how he was and did nothing about it. Wouldn't you rather confess to outright murder?"

Mary-Jo couldn't say, immediately.

"Well then, we had better book a room for him here."

"No," she discarded the advice she had extorted. "He has to be at work to-morrow. He'd better sleep it off at home. Come on, girl, we'd better be going. I'll be with you in a minute."

Julia led the march back to the bar, pausing first, tucking in her bottom and reaching back a prudent hand to make certain that nothing was being revealed that had better be concealed. Then she stuck her chubby, uncontradictable chin in the air and with a final flick to her creased skirt, advanced.

She resumed her seat, looking like the chairman of a returning jury.

The barman, polishing his counter, breathed soft relief as he watched Mel leave, walking with dignity for three steps, then slumping between the two mature ladies who bore him away with strength and desperation.

They held him in the open doorway while the cool autumn air revived him briefly and they withdrew slightly, thinking he could walk alone, but with the second step he stuck his toe in the grating and they were just in time to catch him. Julia, startled out of her disapproving silence, swore and in turn startled the sedate people in the foyer who were watching with discreet sympathy the brave way she bore her burden. Mary-Jo's apparent detachment invited no sympathy.

Julia swore a second time when, having unloaded Mel into the back seat of her own car, she slammed the door and instead of closing, it bumped softly and gently swung open again. She looked down for the obstacle and found Mel's leg slung out of the doorway.

"Lord, I nearly took the foot off him." He groaned as she dragged up the stray but still attached foot and more annoyed with him than ever, flung it into the car and closed the door on him.

Mary-Jo guided her through the city, warning her of traffic lights and one-way streets. After Inchicore she sat back and leaned her head against the window, the tangled irritation of her mind frozen at last with tiredness.

She must have dozed; Julia called her and rapped her knee as they drove across the Curragh. Her tired eyes were hurt by the unshielded lights of the oncoming cars.

"What's up?" she asked, resentfully rubbing her knee where Julia's cumbersome souvenir ring had stung her.

"Have a look back there and see if he's all right. He sounds as if he's strangling."

Mary-Jo twisted around and knelt on her seat. Mel was cramped in one corner of the back, their parcels taking up the rest of the seat. His head was turned awkwardly, his chin stuck in his shoulder. His breathing was alarming. She gripped the lapels of his coat and tried to heave him up into a better position. The car bounced flippantly over a bump and he slid from her grasp.

"You'd better stop."

Julia veered off the road and they jolted and rolled over the wide open grassy plain.

"Men," she said as she jerked to a halt and Mary-Jo looked at Mel's drowned face and silently apologised for not having managed to steer him clear of Julia's ultimate derogation.

As Julia stepped out onto the grass, Mel opened his eyes. "Where are we?" he asked.

"What's he saying now?' Julia asked irritably as if he had pestered her for years.

"He wants to know where we are."

"Tell him we're crossing the Alps. With Hannibal."

Mary-Jo handed out the parcels and Julia took them back to the boot.

"She says we're crossing the Alps."

"Ah that's grand," he said with sleepy contentment.

"So long as we're not going home."

"Why? Don't you want to go home."

"We went home once too often, yourself and myself."
He looked at her through half-deadened eyes, then his
head drooped again. His hair fell across his forehead and
after a moment she reached out and lifted it gently back
into place, but it fell forward again immediately.

"What could we do when they came looking for us?
I'd better get out and give Julia a hand."

He looked up at her and she wasn't sure if he knew her.

"Julia? Is she with you? Jo? You wouldn't . . . . throw
me to the lions, would you?"

"Well, is he awake?" Julia called. "Come here and
open the door."

Julia knelt on the edge of the seat and vigorously re-
arranged him. "His hair and everything," she complained
as she dug her fingers into it and pushed it back off his
face, subtly transforming his rakish appearance to one of
youthful austerity.

Out on the road again, Mary-Jo huddled in her own
corner. Now and again in the stream of light from passing
cars she would watch Julia's squat form behind the wheel,
her breath bated with efficient philanthropy as she
rhythmically dimmed the lights for every oncoming car,
her busy, stubby little fingers excitedly in touch with the
switchboard of the entire world around her. The sight
oppressed her.

In the back seat Mel snored mindlessly, as he was borne,
unconscious and unresisting, back over the miles he had
travelled that morning with such irreversible resolution.

Devotions

LOOKING ACROSS the fields from the road you can see the shrine. A halo of pale light glimmers above the head of the statue. Then it is lost to view again as you leave the road and drive down the narrow laneway that leads to Ladywell. It has been a place of pilgrimage for as long as anyone can remember. . . .

It was the first Sunday in September. The bushes were heavy with clusters of unripe blackberries. Strands of hay which had been plucked off the passing loads trained from the briars.

"You'd want to pump that back wheel before you go home," Ena said to your mother as they pushed the bicycles up the hill.

It had a slow puncture but there hadn't been time to pump it, because Ena was waiting for you in the town.

"We'd better put in an appearance first, or she'll think we're not coming," your mother had said and sent you to close all the windows and to make sure there wasn't a cat in any of the rooms. "It's easy for her to be ready, she has no care on her. If she has sense on her side, she'll stay that way too. I hope that'll be safe till we come back," she said, going in for another look at the fire which she had clamped down with wet slag. "I suppose that other pair took the good pump. What time did they go?"

Chris and Joan had waited until your mother had gone to the Women's Confraternity.

"Not that it would kill you to come to the chapel either," she had said as she fixed her hat. "The prayers there are every bit as good as what you'll say in Ladywell.

But of course you'd rather be off gallivanting on your own. Whatever you're after..." she'd add on the off-chance that they might tell her. They told her they had promised Stella they'd go with her because she didn't know the way.

"Her mother is sending her to get a bottle of the water," Chris added.

"Very well," your mother said, only because one devout woman shouldn't raise doubts about another. "But don't stay around the roads all night."

On this, for once, Chris could give her her wide-eyed assurance, because Stella, she said, had to be home at half-ten at the latest. And Joan ... Joan looked at Chris as if she'd string her up by the heels.

"Well," your mother said, sweeping out her hat-pin, "don't think you're free to run wild around the roads, anymore than Stella Cahill. Remember that, Miss. Be home here at a quarter past ten and not a minute later or it's the last time you'll see out." She looked at her hat-pin and jabbed it in at a different angle. "And before you go, switch that wireless back to Athlone. Luxembourg is a lot of good to me when I want to get the News on Monday morning. Half the country could be wiped out for all you'd know." Dissatisfied with the standard of both religion and nationalism in her household, she went out.

"You and your big mouth," Joan said and went off upstairs to get ready.

Chris, in order to demonstrate that pleasure didn't dissipate her zest for work, had taken on the washing-up. Now finding herself wading through it unapplauded, she looked around for help, and you, standing at the door with your mouth full of cake, collected yourself in time and escaped to the garden and to your hide-out up in the apple-tree.

When they were ready to go they came looking for you. You had offered to accompany them but they wouldn't hear of it, even when you pointed out to Joan that she had been very glad to have you on Wednesday when Chris wasn't at home and she wouldn't have been let out at all that evening only that you were prepared to go to Ladywell with her.

"You were very glad to get out, yourself," Joan said. So you just told her to give your kind regards to Denis. She threatened you then: "If you as much as mention him . . ." You told her that that would be easier to avoid if she'd give over talking about him sometimes. "That's not the way I meant," she said, "and you know it." She watched you, then, wondering if in spite of all the sometimes solemn pacts and the mostly unspoken understanding you might blab to your mother about Denis. She was twice as worried since Wednesday night because now you knew what he looked like. You had met him on the way into the shrine and you all left your bicycles together against the ditch. Denis went on first, down to the shrine, and after a few minutes Joan followed after a while with you and Stella. Which was lucky because the first person you met was Mrs. Drennan who ran the Post Office. She and Kathleen were coming away from the shrine. All Joan was afraid of was that, for your mother's sake, she'd offer to wait and see you all safely home. But Mrs. Drennan and Mrs Cahill weren't talking to each other at the time, so when she saw Stella with you she just said, "Good evening, girls," not looking at Stella, and went on. After an abbreviated Rosary you were prepared to leave, but Denis was still praying. The priest from his parish was kneeling right beside him, that was why. So you all went back two decades and said them again. By the time you had finished, the priest had gone away, and then Denis left too, and you all followed. It was almost dark when you reached the main road. On the way home you and Stella went on ahead and waited at the railway bridge outside the town until Joan and Denis kept up with you. You spent another half-hour there, the four of you talking and smoking Denis's cigarettes while he told you things you'd never have guessed about the people you knew: girls who had had babies, men who beat their wives, and a friend of his who had run off to England with a married woman. Then he told a yarn that made Joan and Stella bend over the handlebars and laugh until they were in agony. Not that you didn't laugh too but they left you so far behind you had to start and think it all out again.

"Nobody can ever find you when you're wanted," Chris said when they had tracked you down in the garden. They had put on their new dresses and had back-combed their hair. That morning while your mother was at Mass they had put olive oil on their eye-lashes to make them long and glossy. That was another of her cribs, that you were never ready all to go to the same Mass. "Mrs. Drennan has Kathleen to go with her anywhere she wants," she'd say. They were wearing lipstick and they were drenched in Apple Blossom perfume which your aunt had brought them from England in July. "Now listen," Chris said. "If Mammy decides to go to Ladywell, and she might if she meets Ena at the chapel, you're to go with them and make sure they go by Knockdrina. We're going by Heywood and if you let her come that way, I swear . . ." She wagged her finger at your face while her beads rattled in its case in her fist, but she made a point of never swearing.

You heard them going; the gate banged after them in the dull still evening. Then the silence returned, the long-drawn out silence of Sunday. The summer holidays were over and you were going back to school the next day. Out on the main road you could hear the whirr of the first cars returning from the match in Dublin. And then your mother was calling you to come on unless you wanted to be left at home on your own.

Ena was waiting for you at the end of the lane in her expensive dowdy clothes, standing beside her stiff shining bicycle which she hardly took out six times in the year. "Did we keep you waiting?" your mother asked, still pedalling on, slowly, serenely, as she sat erect and dreamy on the high saddle. Ena lifted her bicycle to turn it around and in her hurry rapped her shin against the pedal. "Hello, Joan . . . Ann," she snapped, and heaving herself up, flopped onto the saddle and pushed off. One of the men on the corner whistled, causing your mother to dissolve in smiles and blushes and to glance back at you to see what construction you were putting on it. Ena gripped her skirt between her knees and grimaced indecipherably into the sunset.

Your mother explained about the good pump, that Chris or Joan had taken it. "You don't mean to tell me you allowed them to go off on their own?" Ena always expressed her disapproval with a tone of pained disbelief. "Why, won't they be all right?" your mother said. And because you had moved up beside them Ena only muttered something. But everything she ever said about the behaviour of any one of you could begin—Now if they were *my* daughters. Beyond the town again, a hired car passed with a full load, old men and women on their way to the shrine. The one or two who could raise a hand in the crush of the back seat waved and smiled with abashed superiority.

Long before you reached the turning you had cycled on ahead of them, circling on the road while you waited for them to catch up. You turned down on to the Heywood road, knowing that then Ena would find some reason for going the other road not to play into your hands but because she thought it a necessary part of your upbringing to be made to do whatever you didn't seem inclined to do. You heard them calling you back and there they were, standing on the road above waiting for you. "Come on, girl," your mother said, "you're delaying us and we're late enough as it is." You fell in behind them again, watched the shine on the heels of Ena's black patent shoes, pleased with your success. They walked all the steeper hills and, pausing at the top before going on, they looked across at a farmhouse on the side of the hill.

"The one further up, is it, with the trees to one side of it?" your mother asked Ena for your benefit. "It's a fine looking place, all right. That's where Jack Hyland lives," she told you, seeing that Ena wouldn't mind. "You know Jack, don't you?" Ena simpered and twisted the handgrips and began to walk on. "You never know, now," your mother said as they got up on the bicycles again. "We might be calling in to you for tea when we come next year."

Seeing there was no future for you in psychology, you gave yourself up to the pleasure of the moment, free-wheeling past them down the hill, the silken breeze lifting your hair.

"I don't see the other pair, do you?" your mother whispered as you knelt at the shrine. "They must have come the other way, that's a busy road, I hope they mind themselves. Well, get your Rosary said and we'll go. Did I give you the bottle to carry?" It was at home, on the windowsill; she didn't believe you'd forgotten it. "There's Kathleen Drennan getting a bottle of holy water," she whispered, "and making no faces about it, either."

When Mrs. Drennan and Kathleen were ready, they came down and knelt beside you, waiting so that you could all be home together. Kathleen sat back on her heels beside you. "Do you see who I see?" she hissed, watching your face. "R.K.! I bet you were watching him!" You turned away and stared at the remote face of the blue and white statue. "Anyway, he was watching you." But Kathleen was in your way. When you knelt upright so did she. Now you sat back on your heels and as she was about to follow suit her mother looked around and Kathleen was transfixed until her mother was prayer-borne again. In the meantime she would reach back, snatching at your dress to haul you up beside her.

But you had a clear view now. With your face set devoutly towards the statue, your eyes could slide to one side until you could see the maroon shoulder of his jumper and the pale blue collar of his shirt above it. His face was pale and bony and his hair was dark brown and hadn't been cut since school closed in July. You blinked and he disappeared. He too had sat back on his heels and was looking over at you behind the backs of dependent grandparents, widowed mothers, aspirant wives and vigilant neighbours. Then Kathleen plopped back between you and your mother glanced around to see what it was all about.

You tried to rub the criss-cross marks of the damp grass off your knees as you stood up. Ena carried a second headscarf for kneeling on. The holy well was in the centre of the enclosure, in front of the statue. On a bench beside it there were several containers for the holy water. But the men who looked after the shrine were standing in the shelter near the entrance, talking about the match, and the buckets were empty. "Here," Ena said, thrusting an enamel jug into your hand, "run down the steps there and fill that." Your mother reached out to hold your raincoat for you.

There were seven steps, steep and slippery, down to the well. You edged down sideways, the jug tapping every step as you descended. As you reached down to dip the jug you could hear Ena's voice above. "Jack," she called, "you're neglecting your job here." "Say that easy," he said, "or they might stop my big salary." He came down a few steps, and crouching above you, took the full jug and left it on the ground above. "Jack fell down, and broke his crown," he chanted, and tilted forward as if he'd topple into the well and your foot slipped back. He grabbed your wrist and hauled you up. "Steady up, there. It must be poteen is in that spring. No wonder all the ould ones are going mad for it, nipping across the fields, day and night, with their little bottles tucked up their sleeves." He steadied you on firm ground again. His own face was as solemn as a high priest's, but Ena who knew him well and would marry him when all else had failed, looked from one of you to the other and took the holy water away from you.

Ena sloshed the silvery cold water into tumblers for you all, and then as if demonstrating for the heathen how the ceremony should be performed, she dipped her delicate fingers and catapulted a spray of water towards her bosom. "That'll put the run on all the little Devils," Jack whispered to you. Ena blessed herself and three times she sipped the water, saying a Hail Mary each time. Jack,

56

foregoing further edification, had picked up two buckets and gone down to fill them in the well. Ena had a blue Milk of Magnesia bottle hidden somewhere about her and now she took it out and filled it and hid it as mysteriously again.

Afterwards they had stood around talking with women from other parishes, introducing their daughters to each other, and a lone son who stayed in the background, scowling. They discussed you all, whom you resembled, how you had all grown in the past year, the work you did for them at home and what you'd be when you left school. At this meeting of mothers, Ena held her own by talking about her nieces until Jack re-joined you. He had been talking to your mother earlier, telling her his troubles, while she only laughed at him, leaning on his arm and telling him it was necessary to turn a blind eye on many a thing in this life.

"Isn't old Dick Kirwan looking well," someone said, "considering his age. Is that the grandson with him?"

"Indeed, you don't feel the years."

"There's a grand young fella for you, now," Jack said as they passed you on the way to their car. "I saw the other two ladies here, earlier, with the young Cahill one. Coortin' strong, every one of them. What'll happen if the old lady there finds out. She'll have you all locked up in a convent."

He and Ena drifted together on the edge of the group and whenever he caught your eye he'd wink or make a long-suffering face behind her back but he didn't try to extricate himself. They stayed there when the rest of you had said good-night; Ena told your mother she'd meet her in the morning at work. Then you trailed back across the headland in single file; the ripe corn, bowed under the weight of the week's rain, brushed your skirts as you passed. It was almost dark and Mrs. Drennan switched on her flashlamp and they picked their steps carefully, holding each other by the arm and lamenting when one of them stumbled on the bumpy ground.

Out on the road home two men passed on bicycles, one

of them, Denis, leading a third bicycle. The car had passed already with Chris, Joan and Stella hiding in the back, you knew, and when you reached the edge of the town and were about to say good-bye to Mrs. Drennan and Kathleen, you met Chris and Joan about to part company with Stella.

"This is grand now," your mother said, "we'll all be home together."

The Weight of The World

SHE SAT brooding in the corner of the deep windowsill, her bare arms wound around her legs, her chin resting dejectedly on her knees. There were marigolds in a jug on the windowsill too; she had pushed them over to the far corner and now she stared at them in their vibrant colours of orange and gold as if she might divine their secret of resilient life, but even as she watched, their mystery seemed to darken them and her sullen eyes slid away.

Milo crossed the yard, carrying the lid of a churn and singing. When he saw her inside the window he tossed the heavy lid and balancing it on the flat of his hand, held it near his shoulder; he threw out his other arm in a gesture of Latin abandon and releasing all the yeasty passion of his soul into his song, he swooned about the yard and bellowed: "It's now or never, my love won't wait"; and with a sidelong leer he passed by.

She made no response. His good humour, infrequent, and, when it did come, extravagant and hardly ever for an obvious reason, put her teeth on edge. A thousand times he had brutishly trampled her own enthusiasm. Since they had both grown up it hardly ever happened that their good moods coincided, and if they did, it never ended well.

She eyed the door as she heard her mother's footsteps outside and when they passed by she relaxed grimly. You didn't want your mother pursuing you around the house, you didn't want her talking at you all the time, hounding you out when you wanted to be alone and blurting everything out to you. Once you even asked her why she didn't say all that to your father and she said "All what?" as if it were nothing, instead of all the worries that occupied her mind and anyway, she said, he had enough to do and wouldn't want to be bothered; which, you knew, wasn't true. You saw how it saddened him, irritated him, the way she avoided talking to him. And he loved talking to people but not to her. She had been brought up to behave with abject deference to men but in the first years of their marriage her husband had squandered all they had and she had realised that even men were not to be relied on and all her understanding had been confused and thereafter she couldn't even listen to him with respect or without an embarrassed awareness that the source of wisdom and authority was itself a flawed vessel.

The door opened anyway.

"Is that where you are? I thought you'd have come out and said good-bye to them."

"I waved. I don't think they saw me."

"It's as well they didn't. I said you were likely gone up the road with Peggy. I had to make some excuse. Are you not as great with her as you were, or what?"

"Why?"

"I thought maybe since you went away to school and all. . . ."

"You think she's jealous because she hasn't a fairy god-mother too and only goes down the road to school?"

"Well, I hope you know the chance you're getting and make the most of it. There's no obligation on your aunt to spend her money on you."

You turned it over in your mind; it seemed like a good time to tell her that you weren't going back. But you knew very well that just now you were the least of her concerns and you couldn't humiliate yourself by playing for her attention when she was preoccupied.

"You're a handful, everyone of you. Martin, too; fancy him bringing the girl here on a Saturday. It's easy seen," she said with brusque pride, "that fella's turning out to be a real city man. He must think I'm Lady Ormond that I can be ready for visitors any hour of the day."

You wished she'd stop pretending to be annoyed with him.

"Still, we have a lot to be thankful for. Miriam's a very

nice class of a girl, didn't you think so? No put on airs about her, or anything." She said it with faint surprise and seemed ready to reassess herself because Miriam had spoken to her with respect. "And sure, like that again, I suppose they wouldn't be all that much better off than ourselves, just their circumstances were different."

Your Circumstances were a variable measure, the sly foot tipping the scales so that you weren't outweighed.

And as she went on, expanding complacently on what the future could be expected to offer, you turned away. All the while your thumbnail had been chipping away at the indented edge of the cap of the tiny bottle in your hand. You looked down at your right hand now; she couldn't see it – and you held out the brown bottle so that the light filtered weakly through it, making a smoky amber stain on your fleshless fingers. You thought you looked like a corpse already. There were nearly thirty tablets in the bottle. Your mother took two every night to help her to sleep and for months you had been stealing them one at a time. One night you had made her go to bed early and you had brought her her glass of milk and two tablets; only they were Aspirin which you had painstakingly chipped down to the right size. They looked peculiar but you told her your fingers had been wet; anyone else's mother would have screamed and sent for the priest, doctor, Guards and coroner, but she was so overwhelmed by your attentiveness that she swallowed them without a question. You were probably doing her a world of good but you could just as easily have been giving her arsenic. Her unawareness could drive you mad at times.

"Himself's in high good humour," she said indulgently, as Milo, still singing, crossed the yard again. "Have you any idea who he's going with these times?"

"This one, and that one." She couldn't expect two triumphs in the one day.

"He was all pie to Miriam, chatting her up as nice as you like."

You knew; you'd seen it all; it was always an exercise in

61

scepticism for you to watch Milo making himself agreeable.

"I wouldn't mind but I thought he wasn't going to put
in an appearance at all and I was trying to cover up for
him. That's another thing I meant to say to you —" she was
reproachful now — "I thought you'd have put on a nice
little dress when they came instead of them bits of things
you wear. Wasn't that a grand dress Miriam had, I'd say it
must have been very expensive, there was a lovely cut to
it. And yourself and Milo! Tearing like mad things around
the yard; that was the time for you to wear your jeans, it
might have saved a lot of embarrassment. And the roars
out of you! I was mortified in front of Miriam and I'm
sure Martin must have been ashamed of his life after
bringing her here."

"I'll be quieter the next time."

After dinner you had washed some clothes and taken
them out to dry. You were hanging them on the line;
your mother wouldn't let you hang out your underclothes
at all if she thought there were any men about, and even
when she did, she insisted that you arrange them so that
their nature wasn't obtrusively recognisable. You thought
there was no end to her obsessions. As you were hanging
up your slip, something shot by your ear and whipped the
peg out of your hand. It was an onion. There were
hundreds of them laid out on the gently sloping roof of
the hen-house. There was Milo sitting crosslegged on the
roof, smoking a butt, his outlandish wide straw hat
making him look like a Mexican layabout. He knew the
house-rule as well as you did and was tipping you off not
to make a Peeping Tom of him; you picked up the onion
and pelted it at him; it tipped his hat as he ducked; it was a
mistake anyway, all the ammunition was at his side. As
you darted around picking them up to throw back at him,
you stumbled over the hose, snaking down from the tap at
the back-door; you hauled it up and turned it on him. He
jumped up and, crouching, lumbered towards you across
the roof, avoiding the water as best he could. At the edge
he paused and took something out of his pocket; you

couldn't see what it was; he opened his hand slightly, shielding it with his other hand. Something moved, you wavered, the hose in your hand; he knew you detested frogs; you braved it out for a minute; he didn't love them either but often brought in one to make your life scary. Then you dropped the hose and ran and he slid off the roof and came after you, and as you ran yelling past the door your mother came out to see who was going to strangle you, and you crashed open the gate of the haggart and the escaping hens got under his feet and you broke into the garden and he chased you across drills of cabbage and the wet leaves that were probably full of snails brushed your legs and you lifted your knees higher as you ran and you went through the potatoes and was it your imagination or did the blue spray on their leaves sting you; and you launched yourself through the wire fence and into the hayfield that ran around the side and front of the house and there was nothing to hinder you; he couldn't run as fast as you and you had trams of hay to dodge behind, so you rested. Your breath was rasping and your lungs felt like cinders and you put your hands on your knees and staggered around, laughing at his wide trousers and torn check shirt and he said, "Do you see the cut of your own legs, smartie?" And you were plastered with clay up to your knees and you laughed and shouted at each other as you bounded around and he tried to jump over a tram and scattered the top off it and went sprawling through the remains. It took you back years, back to where you had been before they had got the notion and the money to do something about you and have you educated and civilised. And you sat down together and he gave you a cigarette to smoke but when he saw how you took to it he said they'd be bad for you and he took it from you and when you tried to snap it back, he ran off and you went after him and the chase was on again. He led you back towards the house and when he jumped the fence, you took a short cut and sprinted over the wall, your legs and clothes in disarray, your blood-curdling war-whoop lassooing the silence, and there they were.

You stared at the big clean car; you remembered hearing a car but had thought it was your father's.

"Hello, kid," Martin said. He was smiling; if he wanted to he could make them accept you as a likeable tom-boy; but you knew he was surprised, maybe disappointed and annoyed with you.

"Nally!" your mother was bereft of a plausible excuse. And that was Miriam.

You all went in and your mother apologised for the state of the house and said the room should have been done up this year but it wasn't worth while now that you were going to build the new bungalow down near the main road. And instead of sitting down and looking as if she were in her own house, she rushed around straightening cushions, hiding newspapers and trying to rub finger marks off the table-top with the corner of her apron. And all the time she kept looking over her shoulder, thinking that Milo, who had disappeared without a trace, was going to walk in with muddy boots smelling of silage and she was wondering how she'd manage to hunt him out without provoking him to roar at her as he often did and how she'd cover up for his manners. The last time Martin was home he had hit Milo for shouting at her and Martin had ended up across the hearth, his head saved — except that for a minute he didn't recognise his mother — by falling among the sods of turf in the corner; and your mother, unaccustomed to chivalry, asked Martin what he had done that for; and you knew that the trouble with Martin was that he thought that civility and a decent suit should achieve anything and hide everything. With your mother, you wondered where he'd got such an idea. Milo, in his stubborn raggedness, unimproved speech and manners, was twice as arrogant.

You escaped to clean yourself up and you took your time about it.

But you had to go back, and because Martin was watching out anxiously for you, you sat beside Miriam and when she admired your nail-varnish, you admired her shoes. But then your mother, having no notion of the difference between reality and pretence where two unequally favoured women were being civil to each other, leaned over and asked you to agree with her but wasn't that a lovely brooch Miriam was wearing.

"And your ring matches it!" your mother said in the wistful, breathless way she did when she wanted to flatter someone, but the ring was no more like the brooch than the back of a bus and you felt the weight of hopelessness leaning on your mind again and you wanted to escape.

Sometimes when they were fighting, you used to think how nice it would be to have a polite, gracious family who'd sit around making pleasant, unwounding conversation with visitors.

Martin glanced at you with deliberate suddenness and caught the sorrowful look on your face. You could have kicked yourself. You tried to smile but he knew you too well, better than anyone, and he gave a sort of wry smile as much as to say why had you ever thought life would be any different. But you didn't; he was the one who saw the possibility of change and strove for it even though he must have known already that it wasn't going to make him any happier than he had been. For yourself there was only the enervating conviction that if your life began in misery, that was how it was meant to go on, and that belief, almost physically a part of you, undermined every spurt of optimism or ambition that ever visited you and that wasn't much.

You dipped a ginger biscuit in your tea and swayed it back and forth.

"Nally, what are you doing with your tea!" It was the only way your mother took notice of you when anybody was there, drawing attention to your flaws and in the process only highlighting the inadequacy of every one of you; in spite of yourself you jumped and the sodden biscuit fell away and disintegrated in your tea. You began futilely to gather it up on your spoon, your mind screaming hatred at them all for watching you, and Miriam who had helped your mother to make the tea said: I'll get you another cup.

Martin laughed but there wasn't much amusement in it. "Begor, Nal, we wouldn't have turned up our noses at it, many a cold morning we faced out to school with less."

And besides your shame, you felt what he felt always, the depression of remembering, seeing your mother as she used to be on Monday mornings, stooping over the fire of wet sticks that you had helped her gather in the ditches, melting dripping in a pan and giving you a piece of bread each to dip in it. That was the way your mind was too, always slipping and sliding from the expanding comfort of the present to the squalid past.

But in his eyes where there should have been sympathy, there was only tired cold impatience with you because you wouldn't let the memory go and neither of you could as long as you both lived and a glance at each other was enough to reduce everything around you to a mirage that blinded you for a while to the humiliation and poverty that were your real surroundings, because when you were born into it it became part of you, and anything else, anything better, was only temporary scenery. And he was looking at you and suffering maybe; his head tilted back, he was looking down his nose at you and thinking maybe that this was where you parted because you couldn't bear to follow him into the sphere he was entering and what was worse, he was trailing himself into it and now he would always make the story of his humble origins his party piece and you hadn't the pride, or the humility, for that.

And Miriam was smiling at you, the smile of a missionary nun among uncivilised people, that forgave what she had never experienced and could only vaguely understand.

When your father came in, Martin went out with him; he still owned some cattle and it was he who had started restocking the farm. People said wasn't it great the way you'd got it all back into the family and your father looked serene as he went about his work but you didn't see how, when he had had such a love for gambling and the life that went with it, he could be happy without it and be content to stay at home and read the racing news. To you he seemed wraith-like, but then you all did – living differently to the way you had lived before, living better anyone would have said but to you it didn't seem real. And when Martin came home you noticed him noticing the small signs of re-emerging prosperity, and he thought you all took it for granted after all it had cost him but he felt no resentment only an edgy, half amused awareness of his own redundancy.

Your mother and Miriam made fresh tea and just when you thought you could slide back into oblivion, your mother mentioned that your holidays were nearly over and you'd be going back to school. It was as if she wanted it to be known that though you were uncouth now, something was being done about it and they could look forward to an improvement. And Miriam said that since you were in that school you must know this other girl who was her friend's sister. You knew her, a horrible little snob, a tell-tale and at the back of it all a nose-picker which was something even you didn't do. You hated Miriam to think you were breaking your neck to be as good as her and her friends, and you thought it might be as good a time as any to tell them to stuff their fancy school, that you weren't going back, but then Miriam would know that it was because the other girls, ones like her, made you feel like a charity case. But now you felt they had used you enough so you confined yourself to "yes" and "no" and mostly "I don't know" and gradually they forgot about you, you slid out of the conversation and by-and-by, out of the room.

This time you stayed out.

From the windowsill you watched them when they said good-bye; with your mother it was a protracted cere-mony; you saw Martin only half listening to her as he glanced around and you knew he was looking out for you and you saw the strong bleak outline of his face and for a moment you thought you could get up and go down to him but the others were there dealing in bland agreeable talk and you were remembering the first time he had gone away; you couldn't see then how the rest of you were going to survive without collapsing on each other and for a day and a night you had hidden out in a shed; and so you pressed your fists to your temples and you didn't see or hear anything till they had gone.

You heard your father shout "Hup!" as he slapped the last of the cows on the flank as he let them out into the field after milking. The cattle were quiet now; they were new stock, some of them that had been bought at the mart on Friday and all through the night and Saturday morning you heard their lonesome bawling at the gate and the sound could get inside your head until it seemed that the whole world was crying. Now they walked dumbly where they were driven and you were half relieved but sad too as if their resignation had infected you.

Evening wore on; the light changed and the clamour of the yard work took on a different sound, hollow and isolated, as the enveloping noises of the day fell away, one by one.

What's Far Is Fair

IT WAS half past ten again and the breakfast still wasn't completely over. Alice, trying to outface the clock that had counted out every one of the unused minutes of her life, would have liked to turn its face to the wall. Instead, she looked around to see if there was anything she could do now to hurry things up. She heard the tractor coming in by the side of the house and it spluttered to a stop in the back yard. Through the window she watched her husband unloading the churns and then he climbed on to the tractor again. She hurried out and when he saw her he delayed driving away.

"Are you not coming in for tea?"

"You have enough to do. I'm all right."

"Oh, come on in, it's ready and everything."

He hesitated, and finding no sufficient excuse in time, agreed.

"Are they all gone out, or what?" he enquired with carefully suppressed relief as he followed her inside and found, for the first time in a week, that they had the kitchen to themselves. He hung his cap on the back of the chair and began to wash his hands.

"N-no," she said. "Well the children are, but Celia didn't come down yet. Adrian took her breakfast up to her."

He seemed thoughtful as he dried his hands and she watched him — as she spent much of her time doing — trying to interpret his complex silences. "It is their holiday," she reminded him, wondering, without much faith, if that would banish whatever disapproval he felt. He replaced the towel on the roller inside the back door, adjusting it till the edges were even.

"Well, don't tire yourself out trying to look after

everyone. Those youngsters are lively. They'd keep you going." He began to pour his tea, pouring milk at the same time. "Are you having a cup, yourself?"

She moved her cup across the table towards him. "I won't be killed looking after you, anyway," she said, feeling she had misjudged him again. "Why don't you stay in it some morning and I'll bring you your breakfast?" But even as she said it, watching his face, she saw him discard a dozen sharp reminders that he was busy and had work to do in the mornings that could not be postponed.

'Ah, sure you know I couldn't manage that so handy," he said eventually. "Anyway I'd rather be out in the mornings."

"And you won't come with us to-day?"

"Where's this you're off to?"

"I don't know . . . Tramore, or Duncannon, maybe. It's quieter − " she leaned aside to look out into the hallway − "so it's easier on Adrian's pocket."

"O-oh," he said, and she waited hopefully for him to expand on his own observations of her brother-in-law. Adrian was outside, sitting in his rainbow-striped deck-chair at the front door, mistrustfully looking through the local paper, on guard against its non-British stance and insensitive to the jaundiced observation of the few busy people who passed.

"Are you fixed all right, yourself?" her husband asked.

"For money?" she asked and was immediately abashed at having intruded block capitals among the delicate hieroglyphs he dealt in. "Yes, I'm fine. Is that all you're going to drink?"

"That was grand, but I'd better be off. The load of turf'll be ready before twelve."

"I can't see what the hurry is for, to-day. We still have plenty."

"I know that, but I may as well take the load now; it could be dearer later on." He put on his cap, adjusting it with a hand at both front and back before unlatching the door. Then as an afterthought he took some money out of his inside pocket. He left two single notes on the dresser. "Give that to the youngsters. And you'd better have this with you in case you might want anything," he added, leaving a five pound note with it. "Is that all right? What are you smiling at?"

"Nothing, just that I didn't mean he was that much of a skinflint. So you're going, anyway," she said sadly, following him to the door and leaning against the jamb. "Off to lay up stores against the winter. My mother, if she were alive, wouldn't believe her eyes; after all the wasters I struck up with. She said I'd be begging a crust at the neighbours' door, yet. And look how wrong she was. One of us ought to have been able to see ahead and then we needn't have let her die still fearing the worst."

"I don't know." He smiled uncertainly, his eyes fixed on the cloudless horizon. "These things take time to come round to."

That was a fact, she thought, as he drove away, leaving her as unenlightened as ever. Now that she had reached what she hoped was maturity, she often tried to trace the threads of her present life back to their beginnings and she found her own lack of prescience remarkable. She was sure that she ought to have had some premonition that she would marry him eventually. But the only significant thing she could recall about him was that he was always there, even times when she had hardly noticed him.

She thought of all the nights when she or Celia, or both of them, stayed out later than they were allowed to. They'd run up the street to the pub and if they found Dan's car outside they'd sit in and wait for him. At home, their father would march back and forth, from the fire to the door, threatening to have an ash-plant ready if they didn't soon come home. When there was still no sign of them he'd go out to the gate, growing more uneasy with every car that sped past the house on the way from the town; not swearing now, but ridden with guilt for his profanity, having threatened to punish his lovely girls when they were already lying strangled in a ditch some-where along the dark road. And inside, by the fire, their mother would be praying and knitting, perturbed by the draught from the open door, counting the stitches on the needle and getting them confused with Hail Marys. And then Dan's black Prefect would trundle up to the gate and all the wrath and anxiety would be swept away on a wave of relief. Their father, ashamed now of his anxiety, would pretend he had just come out for a tráinín to clear his pipe. Sometimes, to prolong the peace if it seemed more fragile than usual, Dan would come in with them and stay a while, though he wasn't above telling them off himself when he disapproved; and for that, between themselves they called him Uncle Dan.

Then just as they were gaining independence and it seemed to Alice that life was opening out nicely before them, Celia decided to go to England. For one thing, she had concluded that Alice wasn't about to do anything wild enough to justify her vigilance, or remarkable enough to reflect some glory on her. But more than that, she was searching for romance, something unique and exclusive, and not the camaraderie of parish socials, Sunday excursions to Killarney or Connemara, and Saturdays spent shopping in the town; while Alice as yet saw no reason why one couldn't have both.

"I may as well go," Celia said slyly, "because it doesn't look as if Dan is ever going to budge."

Her mother smiled complacently, certain that Dan was manfully hiding a noble love for Celia who, fifteen years younger and with her eyes fixed on faraway places, was beyond his hopes. Her father only said "Hah!" in a disparaging way. Alice saw how it irked him that Dan, whom he loved and respected and had almost reared long before she or Celia or even their mother had come into his life, should be cast by them in the role of forlorn suitor. Not that they didn't like and respect him too, but ultimately they would judge every man on the plausibility of his aspirations. So when Celia tacked on skittish post-scripts to her letters from England: Give my regards to Uncle Dan, Alice ignored them, and if she had anything to tell her, referred to him as Dan Loughlin.

The summer that Alice finished school, Celia brought home her first Englishman. He was such a detailed amalgam of all the qualities which Celia and her mother had down the years decided on as being desirable, if not essential, in a husband that Alice thought he was a joke. Celia had proved that there was in the world at least one strong, good-looking, hard-working young man who was also sober and attentive; who would admire her mother's hat; who wasn't ashamed to walk up to Mass with her and go into the pew at the women's side of the chapel beside her; who'd hold her hand coming down the street in daylight and didn't even wish to join the other men around the lamp-post on the corner while she went home to get his dinner ready; who'd sit unrebelliously among her female relations, and lacking first hand experience, try at least to describe for them how his mother made dropscones, grew geraniums or treated her corns.

Now that Celia had proved that such a man existed, Alice waited for her to catch her eye, burst out laughing and come back next time with someone more believable. But Adrian came the next year and the next. And when people asked Alice was it true that Celia was going to be married, and she said she was, they'd say: And to an Englishman, I believe. Yes, that's right, Alice would say. And they'd look impressed and say, I'm telling you, now! as if it were something remarkable. When enough of them reacted in that way, she stopped thinking, So what? and began to feel that Celia was doing something that not everyone could achieve. And Adrian, five hundred miles away, acquired an aura of exotic romance.

Alice's own life was affected too. When her romances didn't go well – and they hardly ever did though she never knew why – and when whoever she was going with didn't show up for a date, or came too late, or drunk, or with no money to take her anywhere, or on the wrong night, her mother's knitting would pick up speed; she'd sidle closer to the fire and her breathing would change. And Alice would know that she had something to say but was wondering if in the long run it might do more harm that good. But even as she turned it over in her mind, she blurted it out as if her tongue had no patience with her scruples.

"Lord! there's a lot to be said for Englishmen, all the same." And as the years passed and other examples of Irishmen's negligence came to light, she'd shake her head and say, "You won't hear of Adrian doing the like of that."

Not that Alice wished to. By then she had come to respect the hedged wisdom of Celia's direct approach and she recognised the diminishing depth of her own belief that her uncharted drifting from day to day followed some predestined course. When her mother died and Alice gave up her job to stay at home, she felt now at last her lack of ambition had led her into a backwater from which there would be no escape. But there she settled, unresisting and without expectation.

Years later her father died and for a time it looked as if she might die too. Preoccupied people paused to say to each other that it was no wonder she caught pneumonia. How often had they seen her out in the yard at all hours of the night, looking after a sick animal, maybe, while her father, in bed or sitting by the fire, shouted endless orders and demanded detailed reports.

She recovered, and when she came home she found that Dan had sent in a woman to clean the house, curtains had been washed and floors and furniture polished. He had fires lighting in the rooms and when she went around the yard she saw how all the work had been done with his own while she was away, and everything was organised as it had been before her father had grown old and stiff and intractable. Friends called in to see her and when they and Dan had all gone home, she sat alone by the fire in the silent house late into the night.

Next morning, when she awoke, the cows had already been milked and one of Dan's men was driving them down to the fields. Later in the morning the post arrived with a letter from Celia to say that they were moving to a bigger house and now at last she must come and live with them – at least she must come for a holiday and when she found that she liked it she could make permanent plans. It was easy to reply that she would look forward to that and she made vague plans for going in the new year, but the week before Christmas, to nobody's surprise but her own, she and Dan went quietly to Cork and were married there.

In the summer Celia came home with Adrian and their children, and they broke like a spring tide over the house that had for so long seemed settled in terminal tranquillity.

"When you wouldn't come to visit us before," Celia said, "we'll hardly persuade you now."

"Oh you never know. We might go next year."

"Yes, why not! Would Dan come? I'm sure you could persuade him." But earnestly as she said it, her lively eyes skidded away uneasily, and she continued folding the towels and swimsuits that had been drying at the range. She carried them out and piled them inside the back window of the car and sent Adrian to sort out their own children. They were playing ball with a dozen others across the road, and since the ball was theirs and they were taking it to the beach the whole team had to disband.

"It's a pity we can't bring them all," Alice said.

"It is, but we must have a picnic for them some day, somewhere near. Did you say anything to Dan about having a party?"

"N—no, I didn't say anything yet, but it's all right."

"Are you sure? He won't throw you out – filling his house with drunken, midnight revellers? You know, we could ask the Kearnses, they'd supply the music. And we'd have the food ready that day . . ."

And still detailing what they'd give their guests, they packed into the car.

"Dan is not coming?" Adrian checked before closing the door.

"No," Alice said, suddenly impressed by the unlikelihood of it.

"How will he manage for meals?"

"He has relations he goes to when he's up there . . ."

But she stopped at that because Celia, sitting sideways in the front seat, was waiting, patient but preoccupied, her right index finger resting, delayed at the third finger she had ticked off on her left hand. When Alice had stopped speaking and nobody else interrupted, Celia narrowed her eyes as if she had only then begun to calculate.

"And as well as that we could have plenty of tarts and things."

"Sounds like the place to be," Adrian said shyly.

Celia rapped his arm then ticked her fourth finger.

The Followers

"FOR HEAVEN'S sake," Celia said in her unaccountably refined accent that made Alice want to apologise to all the plain-spoken people who had to listen to her. "Don't they ever talk about anything else?"

Four hours after the match had ended she was edging her way, carrying three glasses, through a roomful of preoccupied men, brushing, sometimes bumping against their unresponding peripheries. She set the drinks down on the table.

"Where did you leave the lads?" Pheenie asked with a laugh that was getting sharper every time she tried it and was turned on her own culpable enslavement as much as it was against the unshackled men.

"They left me," Celia said and put down the vodka she had been about to taste. On consideration, she wasn't prepared to let her resentment be drowned or wafted away, so she sat back in the corner to nurse it in unmoistened silence.

Alice was leaning forward, her arms on the table, her eyes shining, eager to be part of the celebration. As she moved to pick up the fresh glass of orange, she became aware of the solitariness of her position and quietly she eased herself back until she was more or less in line with the others, whose attitudes were devoid of enthusiasm.

As far as she could see the only wonder was that Richie hadn't cut loose from Celia much earlier in the day. After the match, when everyone else was crowding onto the field to get near the players and maybe to carry them on their shoulders, Celia had draped her raincoat over her arm, taken Richie by the elbow and conducted him away, out through all the grinning, flag-waving people they knew who were waiting for the last, the triumphant scene, and they joined the exodus of losers and neutral spectators who had begun to stream out a minute before the match had ended when the result was already irreversible.

"Jay, we might as well have lost," Richie wailed, sticking his heels in the ground, when he saw himself being led away from the climax.

"We've had enough of it. What else is there to see? Come on!"

"Celia! Richie!"

Pheenie Walsh looked down into their faces, one impatient, one hopeful. She was standing, five rows above them and launched herself down towards them, the heels of her sandals clattering on the steps. One sandal flew off as she flung herself into their arms in the blind enthusiasm of reunion.

"When did you get back?" Celia asked.

"Oh, yesterday evening! Hello, Alice. Thanks," she said, holding out her hand for her new sandal which already had the five graded stains of sweaty toes on its insole. "Just in time to meet the team as their train came in!"

"Oh the hard man – Tom," Richie exulted, defying Celia. "It was the last thing he said that morning before the wedding: 'Don't worry,' he said, 'whatever else'll be back, Spain or no Spain, I'll be home for the final. Depend on that.'"

"If we were half as dependable," Pheenie said, still in spite of herself lost in wonder at Richie's tact and Tom's devotion, "for getting to the Church on time."

"He was there before yourself, all the same. Isn't that all that's wanted."

"Yes, but only because of my own foresight. Anyway, tell us, did anything wild happen at home since? How's everyone?"

"Oh, all right," Celia said, "but where is he now?" She glanced around with disapproval.

"He's gone in on the pitch," Pheenie said, looking around too, but laughing. She could see Tom's head three inches above everyone else's. "He's easy to keep track of, anyway. He wants to be the first to get the captain on his shoulders. It'll be an uneven ride for the poor devil."

Richie looked back forlornly.

"You're not going away already, are you?" she taunted him. "Sure they're all gone in there now, all the lads. The fun is only starting."

"For whom?" Celia asked.

"Ah, it's a bit of sport, girl."

"Yes, and a bit of sport goes a long way."

And delayed but undeterred she steered Richie away with her. Alice agreed to stay with Pheenie and wait for Tom, and for the rest of the evening she was free from the chill of Celia's disdain and detachment that always forced her to question her own enthusiasm.

It was Pheenie who spotted Richie's car outside the hotel.

"Trust Celia," she said, "to get away from the vulgar mob. Come on in and we'll surprise them. Will you look behind!" she said. "They think we've found a shebeen." One by one several other cars had dropped out of the sober, homebound stream of traffic and nosed expectantly into the car park beside them.

They found them in a quiet corner of the lounge. The eight o'clock news in Irish was on television and Richie was leaning forward, hungering for some scene or mention of the match. Celia, as complacent as an animal lover who's willing to let the dog sniff around all the bins, trouser-legs and lamp-posts he likes as long as she has a grip of the leash, was relaxing. She began by watching the other people, but finding them less fascinating than herself, she adjusted her bracelet and watch, smoothed the legs of her slacks, leaned her head to one side to judge the cut of them, pulled her jumper down to its full length over her waist and held it at her hips and surveyed her figure in perspective.

Her expression of sleek satisfaction curdled when the glass door swung open and she heard familar voices and familiar names. The door closed again and the next time it swung in there was a man attached to it and he was followed by several others and they crowded in beside her. Richie tried to look as if the intrusion were the last thing he'd have wished for. On her other side an elderly arm in gaberdine wrapped itself around her shoulders and the smell of Guinness, sweat and Brylcreme enfolded her as their exuder asked what she had thought of that for one powerful match.

When the News ended, someone switched off the set and the few people who had been there all the time, finding themselves out-numbered, looked to one another for leadership. But when drinks were put into their hands by indiscriminate head counters, they either submerged themselves in the party or disengaged themselves without fuss. Richie stretched out his arm for a pint and there, as far as Celia was concerned, the excursion ended.

After that, she moved around the room, lodging on the fringe of one group or another but they all kept on shifting and changing and nobody wanted to be pinned down. Even as she spoke to somebody, he'd grow uneasy and as soon as he could he'd interrupt, and say "Oh, there's Peter, I didn't see him since morning. Hold on there a minute, I'll be back. I must go and hear what he has to say." And Alice was in the thick of it, lapping it up, with that gullible smile on her face. Pheenie was treated with distant deference and Tom was being feted lavishly. "You know," they said, fulsome with relief, "some fellows'd have gone straight home after and they'd be there now showing the photos of the honeymoon to the mother-in-law or gathering up the bits of string off the wedding presents."

"And what's wrong with that?" Celia asked.

Isolated in the midst of the crowd she wondered who was there she could join up with.

"Cel-yah?" The voice crept up on her.

"And-rew?" she echoed. Wherever she went, sooner or later he appeared there too.

"Hhh-hh," he tittered as if an opportunity was something he wasn't to be blamed for. Holding the knot of his

tie, he wriggled and stretched his neck out of his collar as
if to show her that with a little effort and encouragement
he could be tall enough for her. "Can I get you a drink?
Brandy? Anything you like?"

"Drown yourself in it," she hissed and dived into the
crowd. She grabbed Alice and stayed beside her from
there on. Eventually they were joined by Pheenie and
together they drifted around, too many now to be
absorbed into any group without influencing the tone and
inevitably changing the theme of the conversation, and
there the purpose of the party would be lost.

So gradually they found another seat in a corner, where,
like sediment, they sank, while above and beyond them
the sea of men slowly swayed and swirled around in a
constant seething current of movement and voices from
which intermittent splashes of laughter broke here and
there on the surface.

"Mind if I sit here, girls?"

"No, Kathleen. Hello."

She sat down beside them, her hands clasped hopefully
around her knee as she watched the crop of men, clustered
in enticing bunches all over the room.

"Another refugee," Pheenie said. "Who are you
with?"

"I'm on my own. I got a lift with some people." Then
she resumed her shop-window model's stare across the
roomful of men. But presently, as their immunity to her
persisted, her eyes darkened with puzzlement and an only
half-conscious awareness that somehow things were not
coming to the customary climax. She glanced at the other
three and wondered what they were waiting for.

"You can always take them back and exchange them,"
Celia was advising Pheenie who had got five weighing
scales for wedding presents.

"I'd hate to do that."

"Well, you should have made a list then and let people
see what you needed."

"Ah sure what harm," Pheenie said, sorry that she had
brought up the subject. She wished she could sit there by

herself just listening, and watching all that went on, her mind idling so that she didn't feel time passing. But sitting beside Celia, she had to say something. One silent woman was an enigma, or could be, if there was a man watching with the acquired imagination to think so; two or more tight-lipped women in a corner looked like the hatching of a campaign of opposition.

"Do you colour your hair?" Kathleen asked her without preparation.

"I do not," Pheenie said, stroking it and feeling no change in it.

"I just thought it's staying very dark."

"I haven't it all that long," Pheenie said reasonably.

'You mean it's a wig! Gor, you'd never know; it's terrific. Honestly."

"No, dear, it's not a wig. Little rip," she said to Celia when Kathleen's attention wandered again. "She'd have you on the pension, the first tooth you lost."

Celia, who had all of hers, deployed them in a smile.

Kathleen's invitation was still dangling and getting no bite. This time she lighted on Alice.

"Where did you buy your jumper? I saw ones the very same, piles of them, in Dunne's last week. But they must have been only in children's sizes or something. Honestly," she complained to them all, "I could hardly get one to fit me across here." Her polished finger-nail flickered back and forth across her chest. "And you hate to be too prominent," she confided.

"Sure you must be mortified," Pheenie said.

The last drinks were being served. Kathleen abandoned her passive tactics, moved into the arena and attached herself to her prey.

"Well, ladies, what are ye having?"

"The time of our lives," Celia said as Tom, lungeing and bobbing through the crowd, toppled forward, and steadied himself against the table.

"Isn't it a great bloody night! Are ye enjoying it?"

"Immensely."

"That's good, that's good," he approved guilelessly.

"Ah, there's nothing like it. It's the only night of the year."

"Indeed," Pheenie said, borrowing some of Celia's acid.

"And yourself, you're enjoying it as much as any of them," he said to Alice.

"Her first night out," Celia said, "she'd enjoy anything."

"And are you not having anything better than that!" he asked, picking up her glass of orange, as if something had gone very wrong with her initiation ceremony. He turned to look at the shelves of the bar for the right prescription for her. "Would you try a gin and tonic! That's a nice drink now — all the women take it. Or a glass of sherry!" he suggested, knowing it was what she'd have seen her mother drinking at weddings and christenings. "Aye, a sherry. Now that wouldn't harm a baby."

"Babies don't run the same risks," Celia said as Alice was tremulously about to accept. "She'll have orange, again."

"And so will I," Pheenie said. She was sitting back, her arms wrapped around herself, her bare feet spread on the loor to recuperate, and she assessed Tom, calmly, without a wisp of illusion. "And we're going home then. Now go and get the drinks. How many times," she said when he was gone, "have I sat in a corner watching that fellow going the rounds getting more sloshed with everyone he meets, and more talkative with every drink, and then I have to sit into a car with him driving home taking both sides of the road. Well, I won't complain this time. We're married now. After ten years. I've done my stint, trailing around after him to every dog-fight in the country. Well, this time next year, if God is good and Tom is willing, I'll have a good excuse, or maybe two — did you know that twins run in his family! — to stay at home and watch it in comfort on television. I can sit down with a pot of tea and an apple tart, I'll put my feet up on another chair and I can read the Sunday papers during the dull bits. And Michael O'Hehir'll be there, nice and helpful, to tell me who's scoring and what it is he's scoring and I need never again make an ass of myself above in the Hogan stand, trying to get into the spirit of the thing, jumping a foot off the ground and roaring 'A goal, it's a goal' only to be hauled down and told not to disgrace all belonging to me, that it's a point and Tipperary scored it. And when it's over I can go for a walk or read a book and when I'm tired I can go to bed instead of sitting here getting smoke in my eyes and ruining my kidneys with orange squash."

They were the last to leave. Richie was standing on the steps, forlornly watching couples packing into cars and driving away, cheering each other on the hooting horns, and yahooing through rolled-down windows. His coloured paper cap was askew on his dewy head and on the lapel of his coat the naked legs of a minute doll cavorted below her dishevelled paper skirts. Celia passed by him without a word on her way to Pheenie's car. Pheenie paused to pat his sad cheek and to arrange the doll's skirts more decently, and to tell him that he couldn't win them all.

Made In Heaven

NO. THERE was neither smell nor sound nor sight of fish frying. Three speckled trout he had caught the evening before in an unpremeditated sortie, his first in years, on the preserved waters of the Crainsfort demesne. — You never lost it: he crooned his admiration to himself and lingered for another look before he tucked the newspaper around them and laid them on the floor of the van.

He was asleep before Rose came home, and since she was asleep when he was going out to work, he left a note for her, instructing her in the blandest terms he could command in the knack of gutting trout. Now he found his note, folded over and over and burnt at one end, lying in an ashtray. The kitchen was empty. The kettle was not boiling. It hadn't even been filled. He heard the occasional soft fall of unhurried footsteps on the bedroom floor above him. "Rose!" He called her again, but it was more a lamentation than a summons and only he heard it. He searched his pockets for a match to light the gas. He put on the kettle, reached for the pan but left it where it was and went in search of the trout. He tried the fridge and every press, and stripped at last of all illusion, he opened the back door. The dented chassis of a Hillman Hunter which he had long since pillaged of everything for which he might find a use or a buyer, mouldered in the long grass, a scene of neglect to which he customarily blinded himself. From the houses on either side he heard in stereo effect the same radio commercial; whiffs of cooking flirted for recognition; plates and cutlery clinked on a table; a saucepan clanged on a draining board.

His emergence disturbed three cats who were gathered around his overturned rubbish-bin. The fattest of them, new to the neighbourhood, darted for cover. The others, though tensed for flight, gnawed ravenously up to the last minute. They saw him grab the lid, swing it, and even as it hurtled across the yard and crashed into the side of the car, they were safely on the far side and sorting the spoils they had grabbed. Tim looked down at the mangled remains of the smallest trout. Scraps of newspaper still clung to it. He held his breath to quell the storm of rage, frustration and hunger that threatened to rip apart the fabric of his reason. He went inside and slammed the door and at the sound the new cat came back to her pickings.

Rose's influence on him, it seemed to Tim, amounted to three layers deposited over the years on his consciousness; and it was only at odd moments when in a wishful, aggrieved mood he began chipping away at the accretions of more recent times, that he would glimpse again that first phase and realise the tender, undefended innocence of it all.

Eleven years ago there he was drowning in happiness, laughing with Rose at the extent and diversity of her ineptitude, still chortling over her mistakes as he recounted them at home. "Lord save us, Timmy," his mother would chide him, "you'd want to get something right to eat, whatever else. You can't do a day's work on shop cakes and tea. It's not what you were used to in this house, I can tell you." She would find more and more excuses for Tim to call home, and no matter the hour, she would cook something for him. She disregarded her other daughter-in-law, her eldest son's wife, who would clump around the kitchen, tidying, dusting and polishing everything around her feasting brother-in-law, until he was an isolated blot on the immaculate face of the kitchen. Tim's clear blue unselfconscious eyes would, from time to time, deplore the lack of appeal she had for him as she loomed above him and flicked a dead fly off the windowsill, looking at him as if he'd be the next to go.

Nine years ago his mother had died suddenly.

He sat at the table one evening in early summer and waited for Rose to present him with his supper. He kept his face turned towards the window and looked at the houses on the far side, with their laboriously cultivated flower gardens. Many of the tenants grew vegetables in the plots at the back and a few of them kept hens. Many of the houses had Bed And Breakfast signs of wrought-iron or wood erected at the front gate. Mrs. Nagle, three doors down, kept four lodgers and provided dinners every day for several non-residents. Her next door neighbour was a dressmaker. All the while he contemplated the enterprise of his neighbours he was aware of Rose foostering at the new gas-cooker behind him. The television set was in the corner at the other end of the table. In the blank screen he could see her reflection and, dim though it was, it conveyed the essence of her incompetence. More than the mess she was creating and the awkward inexperienced way she approached the most elementary tasks, what really goaded him was her attitude, her refusal to see the importance of what she had to do, her barely-contained giddiness. At any moment her whim of pandering to him was liable to break up. She'd make a brazen childish face behind his back and stick out her tongue at him. She might start giggling or she could throw a tantrum and tell him to go to hell and get his own tea and what was more to take that cooker back to wherever he had got it, she didn't want a heap of metal taking up space. His imagination zig-zagged over the range of possible reactions, not one of which he would wish to precipitate. He tried to close his mind to her methods, to spirit himself forward to the moment when she would set his supper before him. But even as he lured his thoughts through meandering paths of emollient reasoning the pan of gravy hissed, suddenly, viciously, like a nest of vipers disturbed. At the same instant an egg hit the floor and splashed open. Rose scrabbled after it with a spoon. He saw the covert look she darted in his direction as she did so and he jettisoned all his extenuating arguments. "Sufferinjaysus, woman," he roared as he threw down the knife and fork. "Could you not fry a simple bloddy egg, even. Look at that for a mess, you . . . you slobbrachaun." He caught his breath and waited for the sky to fall in. "Go, clean it up this instant, before I. . . ." Still crouching, she scuttled out by him to the scullery. She brought back a dish-cloth and lobbed it down on the whole broken egg. His stomach surged. A thousand images crashed together in his mind – his mother in a similar moment scooping up the broken egg, putting it in the gallon for the hens, wiping the floor clean in a few smooth strokes, washing her hands and resuming her work – memories of the first two years of marriage unclouded by responsibility. He remembered Rose, one sunny bank-holiday morning, sitting outside on the low wall of the garden. She had been wearing a yellow dress and white sandals. Young and carefree, she chatted with the older women from the houses on either side. He recalled the feeling he had had at that moment, seeing himself suddenly as part of the backbone of hard-working men which sustained this cosy community of laughing, idle women. And then there was the un-articulated decline of the past few weeks.

In the instant in which he raised his hand and bore it down so that it slapped the side of her head and he felt the high cheekbone, the cool rim of her ear, the smooth hard stone of the ear-ring and a strand of her hair under his fingers, he was borne up by a surge of pride. He'd make her change her ways, learn to cook and sew and keep the house as other women did. She couldn't stay young for ever, she must know that; and her looks would fade. The honeymoon was over. A new phase was about to begin, one that could be just as good in its own way. As he drew his hand away from her face, he thought of this as a benediction on her, the stroke on the cheek that confirmed her, fitted her for a new mature role. He felt a kind of serene sanctity flow through him. They'd buy a cookery book. He'd ask Nick's wife for some of his mother's recipes. Mrs. Kearns next door would help Rose through the early stages. He'd be patient and together they'd go forward.

She was still kneeling and he reached down to raise her up. She looked up at him. Her face was pale and taut with a kind of spirituality. "Rose, girl," he said, "this is only the beginning. . . ." Before his eyes, the colour flowed back into her face. Slowly she straightened up, pushing his helping hands off her arms. "Tim Effing Dunphy," she whispered, almost to herself, as if she had difficulty in recognising him. She repeated it in her most refined enunciation. He gaped at her and she flicked his face with the egg-smeared cloth which had been already wet and filthy. She flicked it again and he backed away and she came towards him, flicking it in his face, left and right, in short vicious insulting swipes as they two-stepped around the room until he stumbled back against the cabinet. Despite his shielding arms, she slapped him around the head and neck while he tried not to absorb the smell and smear of the cloth. He was helpless and her words were like a message meant for someone else. "If you think you can start knocking me around. . . ."

"But, Rose, for the love o' . . ." But as he tried to correct her misunderstanding of his intentions, a corner of the cloth trailed across his mouth and he buried his face in the crook of his arm.

"You lousy little rat you."

He managed to slink away into the scullery and close the door between them. When all was quiet, he moved out. In the mirror beside the window he looked at his defiled face and his eyes regarded their reflection as if they would never close again.

That was the beginning of the second phase, an era of mutinous silences broken by frequent bickering, some violence and rare interludes of harmony. But the trend of their relationship was downward until at some stage it had come to rest on a plateau of mutual ironic toleration. From there it could lift off for brief flights, when they lost sight of the disparity of their expectations and shared moments of near happiness, but it had found its permanent base to which it always returned. He might have left her but Damien had been born then and he could not bear to go. A year later Val was born. And yet, it seemed to him in retrospect that apart from the gratifying fact of their existence, the children had made little difference to his life. As often as not he came home to find that they had been left into someone else's house to be minded. In the early days he would rush out to fetch them home immediately until he came to appreciate the exigencies of their presence and then he began to postpone it until he had had his supper, and then until he had read the evening paper or until he had seen the news on television. And besides, he had begun to resume the jobs he used to take on before he had married, working at night, servicing cars, repairing machinery for farmers.

Rose was leading the life that amused and occupied her as before. Her mother lived six doors away, a gaudy widow who got up late and sat around until evening in a vivid patterned dressing-gown, renewing her lipstick whenever she saw anyone passing who might call in on the way back from the shops. She dyed her hair and painted her nails, though that alone would not have antagonised him. She smoked constantly and had a nerve-racking cough which she had refined to such a degree and accompanied with such a cascade of heavily-scented handkerchiefs that healthy people felt crude and green in her presence.

Tim had a poor opinion of the circle of women with whom Rose and her mother mixed. They were people of no property, of no ambition, who yet managed to live comfortable unhurried lives. They spent their days drinking tea and talking in each other's houses, playing cards, breaking off at a moment's notice to make unurgent trips to one town or another to back a horse, see a fashionable wedding, play Bingo or attend an auction, though not to buy; or be the first to enter any newly opened shopping centre, church or lounge bar. They were ready and waiting to turn out to witness a crash, a fire or a row, or get the autograph of a famous person. They committed so little time or effort to what other people considered to be the moral obligations of a working day that they could lavish it instead on the fringe events, activities which amused them and gave them something to talk about, to relate to their work-bound neighbours. To Tim's mind there was something immoral and unwomanly about such an idle, frivolous style of living which he could not reconcile with his own traditional, inbred and instinctive expectation. Young women were decorative and irresponsible and if they were not they depressed him. But he expected them to develop as a matter of course into mature women who were useful and busy, and if face, figure and personality survived the process, that was a bonus one had no right to expect.

Tim drank the scalding tea with careful slurps. Leaving the cup on the table beside him, he groped for his slice of bread and cheese. In his other hand he held a paperback novel open. The road outside was quiet again. A moment before it had swarmed with schoolchildren hurrying back after lunch and there were still a few stragglers. He sat sideways in his chair at the window so that the light fell across his left shoulder onto the page, which was the method his revered schoolmaster used to prescribe. Thus he bandaged and soothed his raw nerves. Even so, he still registered every sound of Rose's footsteps in the room above and sometimes he had to re-read a sentence or a whole paragraph. The bedroom door had opened. – What the hell did you do with the trout. . . . Another door closed; she had gone into the bathroom. There were paragraphs he was going to read again, either way, when he had finished, and as he read one of these his chewing slowed down. His finger would creep in from outside the book and bend the corner of the page. Sometimes it turned down easily as it had been done before and Tim would smirk to himself. Sometimes the page he was about to mark looked as if it had never been touched before and that worried him a little. The bathroom door opened. – That was a grand way you fried the trout. . . . She was back in the bedroom again. Someday the wardrobe would topple over, the way she chucked at that door instead of turning the handle. Sometimes a page was dog-eared and he had found nothing in it so he'd go over it again, combing it for something, a new term maybe that he hadn't heard before. This worried him too, that there might still be something he didn't even know he didn't know. The radio music grew louder as Rose carried the transistor down the stairs. He moved slightly in his chair. — Tell us, did you by any chance see a couple of trout I left in last night. They were in a bit of newspaper. I thought you might fry them for the dinner. . . . The music rose and fell, cleared and blurred, as in moving the radio its direction and position changed. That grated on his nerves too.

He rubbed his fingers on his trouser leg and turned a page as Rose came into the kitchen. She left the radio on the edge of the table and it blared and rasped beside his ear. His eyes skidded over the printed page and he gnawed a crust of bread. She was searching for something under the cushions. He adjusted the radio until the sound cleared.

"That's better," she said agreeably.

"It isn't beyond you to put it right yourself, is it?" he said. And since it had long been his policy to let her be responsible for the first volley, she was surprised. She lifted her head as she stooped over the armchair and looked sideways at him, just like a grazing pony, he thought. She raised her fine eyebrows and he knew that look of broad-minded, patient amusement. But she was dressed for going out and hadn't time to spare. "Oh, you're better at that kind of thing," she wheedled in a routine way. As she searched along the mantelpiece, she looked at her face in the mirror. Her make-up was perfect and she was pleased with her new scent. From her mother and her cronies she had picked up hackneyed, ill-fitting tips on how to handle him. She was too lazy to modify the general rules to suit him and thus he, who felt he could have borne almost any trial, was wounded in his most vulnerable aspect, his pride in his own individuality. Among all the women he had met there had been one or two who, in Rose's place, would surely have recognised his unique worth, and his bruised mind would delve into plangent daydreams of a re-union with one or other of them.

"Is your tea all right?" she asked suddenly.

"Why wouldn't it be?" Under his breath he added, "When you didn't make it."

"What's that you said?"

"Nothing," he said, rustling a page as he turned it. "I said what could be wrong with it, that's all."

"Hah?" she said, going on to search the other chairs. Already she had lost the trend of what he was saying. If he confused himself too, then in retrospect he wouldn't seem so unarguably a coward. All the time he kept his eyes fixed on the book. Three times they had zigzagged over the same few lines. Sometimes they settled as pointlessly as flies on one word but in the context of his own thoughts it would seem foreign and meaningless. Somewhere perhaps such words were used, but only by people who were free and unattached and had no belittling personal difficulties. A man couldn't use a word like piquant, say, then turn around and in the next breath abuse his wife. "Did you see any sign of a cigarette lighter?" she asked at last. "Ettie thinks she might have left it here yesterday." "Was that ould harpy in here again? No, I didn't. Though someone seems to have done a deal of tidying-up." "If you're referring to that . . . parcel," she said, "you can guess where you'll find it. Such a disgusting . . . phew. Don't bring them in here anymore, if you want a quiet life." She had given up the search and was straightening her slacks and jacket. "And that's a filthy old book you're reading. Make sure you put it some place Damien and Val can't get at it. You may forget the top of the cistern. They're able to climb, you know."

When she was leaving he said Good-bye and have a good time. He switched off the radio, put aside his book and sat very still. When he judged she had reached her mother's house he got up and put the pan on the gas-ring. He reached the door in time to take the parcel from the child he had sent up to the town. He gave him twenty pence for himself and said he hoped he wouldn't get into trouble at school. Back in the kitchen, he tucked a tea-towel into the waist band of his trousers. He surveyed the kitchen. He whistled as he moved into action, opening and closing cupboards and drawers, to fetch a plate, a knife and fork, pepper and salt. While the fat was heating on the pan he had opened the parcel, spread the steak on the table and pounded it with a wooden spoon. He had two onions ready, peeled and sliced. Now as he stood by the pan, poised to turn the steak, he looked out at the cool sunny day. He thought over the work he had to do for the rest of the day. And afterwards he would be going out to see Nick. His wife had phoned him; she wanted to have his opinion of a second-hand car Nick was going to buy for her, instead of the new one she wanted. A feeling of self-sufficiency expanded gently within him and bore him up.

Sixpence In Her Shoe

SHE STARED over the edge of the book into the far dark corner under the stairs. A bunch of men's old coats hung there, unconvincingly inanimate, with wellingtons standing on the floor beneath them and a hat hanging above them from a nail on the casing of the stairs. Sometimes the branches of a tree brushed against the window, but she had grown used to it throughout the previous winters and now she didn't look up anymore at the scribbling noise it made.

A spark flew out of the open door of the range. Without looking away from the paper she was reading, her mother-in-law drew her feet back under the form. Helen reached over for the tongs and picked up the charred chip of timber. "You couldn't mind the tiles with them," Mrs. Frewin said, to show she wasn't entirely careless of what was happening around her, though her mind was already straining after a notice that had caught her eye. She flapped down one corner of the paper for a moment to look at the hearth. "I suppose we do wrong to open the door," she said, without having any intention of changing a habit she had acquired long before they had tiled the kitchen floor or made other renovations when Eamonn was getting married, and she shook the paper into position and began to read again. Helen sat opposite, leaning forward, her elbows on her knees and the tongs lying idle in her hands. There were several small holes burned into the tiles but she knew now that the sparks didn't cause them; she had seen how her mother-in-law when she was lighting the fire or stoking it would kneel in front of the range, shaking down the ashes with the poker; she'd rest there, watching the flames before closing the fire-door; then she'd stand up, holding on to the towel rail with one hand, leaning the other heavily on the poker, and the still hot tip would bore into the tiles. Helen was elated with her own detective work. "That's what's doing it," she had blurted the first time. "Indeed, now, I don't think so, girl," Mrs. Frewin had said, as she put the poker back in its place and wiped her hands on her apron. "Sparks are flying out there all the time, what else." And she still used it to help herself up, and still attributed the burns to flying sparks, with sly defiance at first, until she saw that Helen was not going to contradict her.

Helen still called her Mrs. Frewin and though she didn't seem to mind that, accepting it as deference that was due to her, or as awkwardness that would wear away or resolve itself now that the baby was beginning to talk, Helen knew that Eamonn noticed it, and she had no need to look at him anymore to know the irritable, critical look on his face when she wouldn't step down off her perch of self-protective caution and reserve to immerse herself more in the ways and manners of the household. She cared about his reaction only a little more than she had intended to and it was only lately that he had begun to waken to the fact that her self-containment was not part of a game she had devised to intrigue him.

When she heard the sound of the latch of the gate, she raised her head. She glanced at her mother-in-law, but she seemed not to have heard anything. On the windowsill, the wireless was scratching away unheeded on weakening batteries. After the longest delay she could afford, Helen stood up and said, "I think I'll go up and get out something to wear for the morning."

"Right, girl," she said mildly, and when she was halfway to the stairs she said, "Will you just open the door there while you're up and let Mrs. Loughlin in. I thought I heard her step there going around to the back."

"Oh," Helen said with as much innocent surprise as she could raise, and with hesitant query went over to the back door. There was a rap of knuckles on the window before she got there.

"Good-night, Helen," Mrs. Loughlin said in her breath-

less, confidential voice, sliding in between Helen and the
end of the stairs and turning to face the open doorway as
quickly as if she thought there was someone following her
who might still try to stab her in the back. She left a pot
of home-made marmalade on the windowsill and looked
around the partition into the fire corner. "Hello, Nancy,"
she called briskly as if she'd get around to her later. "Is
that yourself?" Mrs. Frewin said, and turned over a page
as if she could wait too.

"Well," Mrs. Loughlin said, unknotting her scarf and
feeling her hair for dampness, "isn't it filthy old weather,"
and while she unbuttoned herself before Helen, she
resumed her confidential tone. "I suppose you're out
working everyday, yourself? Aren't you great! Is the little
lad well?" She tidied her apron under her open coat,
pressed in her stomach with her hands while she looked
down at her feet before going into the kitchen. "Sure
you're all right when you have Granny here to look after
him," she continued, her tone evolving rapidly to one of
raucous teasing. She pressed Mrs. Frewin's shoulder and sat
down on the chair Helen had left. "Well, how are you?"
she asked in a deeply friendly way that discounted all the
other openings of the conversation.

"All right, sure, girl. And yourself?" Mrs. Frewin said
with as much sincerity while she folded the paper and
sharpened the creases of it with her fingers. They looked at
each other, hard eyes softening in hardened faces, and
there was no comforting known limit to the torment
either of them might have been put through since last they
were talking together.

Helen waited around for a while, caught, as always,
between the intrusion or the civility of staying and the
discretion or the hostility of leaving them. She had
brought in the present of marmalade and they had talked
about it, Mrs. Loughlin deflecting their appreciation by
saying they might not be made up with it, she thought it
was too thin compared with the last lot she had made, and
when their undiscerning thanks echoed around them,
silencing them, she cleared her throat, held one hand

before the fire while the other clutched her folded head-scarf in her lap and she said that that was a great blaze they had going and enquired if that would be part of the old apple tree Eamonn had cut up?

"The men are out, then?" she asked, looking over her shoulder.

"Eamonn was going down to a meeting. The uncle Peter went as far as the town with him."

"We have the place to ourselves, so. Aye, well, sure," she said watchfully, extenuatingly, philosophically, for fear they would think she was complaining. She settled the tail of her coat to either side of her, folded her hands in her lap, the warmed one kneading the other, and sat like an obese, obedient schoolchild with her toes straining to touch the floor. Mrs. Frewin sat back, her arms folded, her ankles crossed, her legs sliding closer to the heat, and from the other side Mrs. Loughlin edged closer too. And as they trimmed away the trivialities their conversation began with, their voices would become quieter and unself-conscious. Mrs. Frewin would put another block or a sod of turf into the range and close the door on it while it lit up; she'd reach for the kettle and pull it forward onto the hot plate, lifting the lid to see if there was enough water in it, and tap it on again with her fingertips; Mrs. Loughlin would interrupt what she was saying to warn her to mind herself, she could get a terrible burn that way, and well, where was she? And she'd resume her story, and Mrs. Frewin, listening with the expression of perpetual but unspecific empathy of a statue on a frequented side-altar, would finger the hem of her skirt, easing it absently over her knees as she edged nearer to the diminished, then increasing heat of the fire. Mrs. Loughlin when it was her turn to listen, would now and again rub her thighs, bundling her apron aside, and parting her knees to the limits of her straight skirt.

They'd talk about their families, what they were doing now, which of them had written lately, or who was coming home soon, though Mrs. Frewin always told rather less than she heard. They'd discuss everybody's health, though there again Mrs. Frewin was reticent about her own and her family's; yet if somebody she knew was ill, she'd ask everybody who came near the house if he had heard anything more and what did he think the complaint might be. They'd talk about money. Mrs. Loughlin would complain suddenly about the amount of her electricity bill, or what it had cost to get a pair of shoes mended, or how small their Creamery cheque had been the last month. They'd grouse about the price of everything, and though Mrs. Frewin would seem to talk freely, she never gave away a single fact about how much she had paid for anything or what they had earned with any crop.

Mrs. Loughlin had long ago recognised that Mrs. Frewin did not return confidence for confidence, and with that realisation the first warm burst of friendship which had sprung up between them when they had both come as strangers to live within half a mile of each other, had cooled rapidly. For both of them their first memory of life in this place was of golden peaceful summers. "They were grand times," Mrs. Loughlin would often recall, polishing the picture till the patina of sentimentality glossed over the dull patches and blended them into the bright distant blur; "When the children were small and you always knew where they were." And though Mrs. Frewin felt the same, she could not bring herself to sigh openly for the glorified past and by implication denigrate the prosperous present. But recalling that time, she would always enquire, "And how is the old woman keeping!"

And Mrs. Loughlin would say, "Grand, thanks be to God," her voice taut with earnest suspension of judgement on a God who showed no sign of winding up a life that threatened to drag on till her own was spent. "She's as well as ever," and she'd knuckle her fists into her lap and there would be silence as she reviewed all she had suffered at the demands of the old woman who had cornered all her days since she had married into her house thirty five years earlier. She remembered her as she had been at the beginning when she used to spend all her time working around the yard, looking after calves and pigs and hens and turkeys. She'd come plodding into the kitchen then in her men's wellingtons, her shoulders sloped by the weight of the buckets of feed she always seemed to be carrying from barn to range and from range to trough. As she stood at the range waiting for the mash to heat, she'd light the cigarette that she always had ready drying out on the edge of the range, she'd take a few pulls and then watch the two younger women — Kitty, her daughter-in-law, and Nancy Frewin — red-faced and giggling and hysterical, one at either side of the kitchen table, as they tried to drive a wooden spoon through the big saucepan of jam they were trying to make, whatever efficiency they had acquired vanishing under her unsympathetic eyes. She looked on with time-marking tolerance at her daughter-in-law's efforts to reform their life-style, but as the years went on and she herself grew older and was no longer able to cope with all the yard work, she delegated it, bit by bit, to Kitty who had gradually abandoned her image of herself as a cherubic housewife entertaining her town-pent relatives with home-grown food or doing crochet work in the drowsy afternoon while the bees hummed among the nasturtiums under the window.

And in those early days, as she found the burden of essential work settling on her shoulders, leaving always less time for the fragrant sidelines she had dreamed about, her one consolation had been her friendship with Mrs. Frewin: her husband had no comfort to offer her except his satisfaction that he had married in good time and brought in a woman to replace his mother and to look after her now that she needed care and attention. Whenever she could leave the house, she'd come down for a cup of tea and she'd sit in the corner and look enviously around her at the house Mrs. Frewin had to herself, to run as she pleased and a well-organised husband who had no need of her help in the yard, and his wistful, unmarrying brother, Peter. She'd pour out her troubles, her resentment sharpened by awareness of the contrast and that since she had nobody else, she had to confide in Mrs. Frewin and so add weight to her sense of superiority.

And when Mrs. Frewin would say, "Well, sure, none of us gets it all our own way," she'd agree to be consoled for the time being by vague impressions of hardships other than her own. But it was in roundabout ways, through other people, that she discovered odds and ends of Mrs. Frewin's business that would have evened the score and eased her mind: Matt Frewin's unrelenting meanness; the manoeuvring they did to inherit an adjoining farm; the undisclosed visits Mrs. Frewin made to a doctor in Dublin; all topics which would have kept them in talk for months and taken her mind off her own plight and her gathering conviction that she suffered more than anybody on earth. When it dawned on her that while she had been pouring out everything that concerned her and finding perverse solace in the thought that her life, at least, had some element of drama, Mrs. Frewin had listened to her without ever giving away a hint of her own interests, Mrs. Loughlin had tightened her lips and resolved never to talk to her again. But she couldn't suffer in silence and when she confided in anybody else, the story always came back to her mother-in-law and caused more trouble. So she came to realise that Mrs. Frewin's shut mouth, though it might offend her own concept of mutual friendship, was also a safeguard for her, and on this unequal new basis they became friends again. But the barrier was there, noticeable only when Mrs. Loughlin was chattering away in a realm of gossip below the standard Mrs. Frewin observed for herself. Then Mrs. Loughlin gave the impression that in less restricted circumstances her friends would be other women like herself who told all their worries to anybody who would listen and who had undiscriminating interest in the most trivial detail of other people's existence; while Mrs. Frewin's life would lack its chief distraction since she would not stoop to winkle out the kind of inside information which Mrs. Loughlin furnished unasked.

Now as they talked together about people whom Helen still only vaguely knew, she excused herself, saying that she'd go up to see if the baby was all right.

"I thought you said you wanted to see to your clothes for the morning," Mrs. Frewin said mildly as if she were the forgetful one. Helen said that she had to do that too.

"And you're off to work everyday!" Mrs. Loughlin said, this time the altered phrase making it sound like an excursion.

Helen said yes and Mrs. Frewin said nothing and Mrs. Loughlin said, "Sure aren't you as well off, and all, not to be getting in each other's way. Isn't one of you enough here to do what's to be done! And you won't be like we were," she said with a laugh, "selling a few eggs on the sly to have a couple of shillings for yourself." Warily she watched Mrs. Frewin and they hated each other then as witnesses to and mirrors of each other's exploited time. "And your staff dance is next week, Eamonn tells me. You'll have to let me have a peep at the new dress before I go off. Well, don't let me keep you now from whatever you have to do. We'll be all right here, having a little chat for ourselves," she said cosily, her bleak eyes unblinking as she turned away from the vast emptiness of the kitchen, and noted patiently that the kettle was beginning to boil.

The Pet Of The Family

"LOOK AT that for a sky," Jim Casey said. He released the handle of the pump and the water trickled onto the ground as Fionnuala lifted the bucket away.

"I thought we were done seeing you carrying buckets of water," Mrs. Casey said, coming out again. This time she had her coat on and she was tying a scarf around her head. She tugged at the front door and it locked behind her.

"Don't be long there, you," she said to Jim, "or the storm'll be on top of us. Don't delay now, child. If it was raining fire and brimstone you'd have to be out in it." She hurried away towards the barn, bolting the doors of sheds as she passed.

The first flick of wind skimmed a few straws along the ground towards them. Jim held the gate open for Fionnuala, then slowly crossed the yard. Out on the road, she switched the bucket to her right hand. With her other hand she held the tail of her coat close to her. Water, ice-cold and sharp as splinters of glass, splashed her leg. Her mother had given her no time to change out of her school clothes and to put on jeans. She had met her at the door. "Here," she had said, handing her the bucket," before you stop to have your dinner or anything, you may run over to Casey's for water, there's not a drop in the taps. There's something seriously wrong with that whole system. I know it. And your father of course is off at a funeral and there's no knowing when we'll see him. Now don't make Mrs. Casey any the wiser if she quizzes you."

"There now," Mrs. Casey had remarked as if she had foreseen how it would turn out. "Your grand new house and it all no good. Maybe you were as well off where you were. Do they ever think of coming over to take a look at it? You'd want to tell him there's slates flying off of it like autumn leaves, every gust of wind that comes. You'd be in danger of your life passing it."

"Ah, it isn't altogether as bad as that," Jim commented as Mrs. Casey went in again.

Across the road the house where they had lived until that summer was silent and empty, absorbing the darkness of the evening. Down at the main road they had built a new house; from here they could see the red tiled roof and the white walls. Three times during the building of the house her father had quarrelled with the contractor. At first the men would stay away for a few days. Then some morning they would be back on the site, working as if nothing had happened. But after the third quarrel they stayed away altogether and Mick Gaffney sent his helpers to collect all the tools.

Her father and mother quarrelled then. She asked him was he satisfied now! He said he was; he had never been impressed with the way that that man approached his work. He had watched builders at work here and in England; he had worked with them himself; and it seemed to him that the professionals would take a poor view of Mick Gaffney's methods and ability.

"Professionals!" her mother said. It was enough for her that Mick Gaffney's father, and his father before him, had been builders and Mick had been at the trade since he was high enough to hand his father a hammer. It was in the blood and he had had the training and the experience. But of course if *he* thought he knew better. . . .

He not only knew better, he said; he could do better. Hadn't he worked on buildings all the time he was in England!

"And how long was that!" she said.

"Long enough to meet you," he replied winking at Fionnuala behind her back. And he had learned all there was to know about building.

Wasn't it a great pity then, she said, that he wouldn't apply himself to that trade since farming didn't seem to satisfy him.

"Who says it doesn't! Don't we make a good living

104

from it?"

"We do," she conceded.

He looked up at her, recognising all that she left unsaid. "We do," he echoed, "but we could make a better one, is that it? If I remember rightly, you were the one who wanted to change. It was fine, when you were twenty, to fall in love with a navvy, but once you were married it had to be to a farmer."

She flung down the pillow-case she had been spreading on the ironing-board.

"The farm was here waiting for you," she cried. "What else would you do but come back to it? Or did you want strangers to have it? They've had enough of it as it is, and only we have good neighbours who chip in and keep us from falling behind, they'd have it all. And now instead of getting on with your work and letting Mick Gaffney get on with his, here you are proposing to take on the building. . . ."

"I suppose you think I couldn't do it?" His eyes gleamed.

Her mother had swiftly withdrawn into silence, hoping that if nobody challenged him his new ambition would fizzle out as so many others had done. Then in a week or two she would have a discreet word with Mick Gaffney who, for her sake, would come back and finish the building.

But this time it didn't happen that way. The next day was St. Patrick's Day. At any other time a Holy day coming in the middle of the week would have served to deflect his rash intent. Indeed he always formulated his most ambitious schemes on the eve of a day when no work could be done.

Fionnuala and her mother were home from Mass and had the dinner ready but her father still had not come up from the new building. He had let them out of the car there and they had walked the rest of the way home. Another car drew up at the site as they left and before they reached home yet another had arrived. Later her mother sent her down to tell him the dinner was ready.

There were three men with him. They were standing around, one of them sucking a pipe, another lighting a fresh cigarette from a butt, the third scratching his head as they discussed what had still to be done and how it should be approached.

"Wouldn't you say that'd be the way to do it now, Dick?" one of them asked the chain-smoker.

"Aye, I would, Peter. I'd say that'd be your best tack. Aye, aye." He could no longer hold off coughing. Their agreement on every point was so unctuous it was clear that not one of them had brought to the meeting any personal experience or conviction of any proven theory.

"Will you look at them," her mother said, standing at the kitchen window, "and they wouldn't build a hen-house between them". She was silent for a moment at the prospect before her. Then she began to laugh. She laughed and laughed, leaning her weight on Fionnuala's shoulder. She drew a handkerchief out of her apron pocket and began to mop up the tears from her face. "The Lord look down on us," she said, then braced herself again and put her handkerchief away. "The thousands of pounds that have gone into that. Every last penny we had saved, and on top of that all that Uncle Barney left me. Thousands," she repeated to Fionnuala, as if between them they might grasp some concept of infinity. "One good woman would be worth ten men. She'd have less psalming about what she was going to do, or else she'd stand out of the way and let someone that knows get on with the job. And I have no use saying anything. Who wanted a new house? he'll ask me. Who was never done complaining about this house, that it wasn't laid out properly? It wasn't bright enough. It was too far back from the main road, and the lane was primitive. The ceilings were too high and you couldn't heat the rooms." Overcome with guilt, she recited her own litany as it would sound when her husband charged her with it, and she saw that not one of these flaws was beyond her own power of endurance. She had indeed endured them all for more than twenty years. Her four eldest children were educated and settled in jobs

106

or were training for them. The younger four weren't so far behind. Ten years more and they would all be accounted for, even Fionnuala. Ten more years of patching and painting over the cracks and the dampness. Ten winters of freezing in high, draughty rooms. And fiwhen they were all grown up and gone, what then? "Oh, but you pay for your ambition," she said. "You want to improve things and all you hear is: Aren't you all right the way your are. You don't know when you're well off. Aren't you lucky to have a house of any kind and all the poor people of the Third World who have nothing. Did you ever hear such an argument as that to give me. But here, go down and tell him to come to his dinner, anyway."

"Well, young lady," Peter said when he saw her there, "are you looking forward to your new house?" He seemed to think himself then that the query was premature; while she, her initial excitement wrecked on setbacks and disappointments and finally demolished by her mother's influence, had nothing to say.

"Child's play," her father said when eventually he sat down at the table. "Was I mad or what, going to pay Gaffney that kind of money for a job I could do in my sleep. All I need is someone to hand me things; any of the lads'd help out if called upon."

"And if they have no prior engagements."

"And our own lads'll be home the week after next, or when does that college close for Easter? No matter, no problem there at all. You can be pouring the tea there, I won't stay to argue with you this time. I want to get on, I have calls to make. I want to round up a few implements."

"So there'll be no Parade for us to-day."

"The Parade? Why, were you thinking of going?"

"It's not much good thinking these things on my own."

"Now listen here. Next year we won't have all this work on hand and we'll go see all the Parades you like."

"It's the child I'm thinking of," she snapped. "What would I want with Parades, don't be foolish."

"The child can come with me. We can make our own

Parade, can't we!" He nodded to Fionnuala to go and get her coat before there were any objections raised.

"Well, get on then and let me tidy up before Kitty walks in on us."

"So Kitty is coming over. Come on, pet," he said to Fionnuala.

And so she spent the rest of that day with her father, driving around to houses she didn't remember having visited before. Everywhere her father was welcomed; front doors opened to them before he had switched off the engine and someone would come to meet them and usher them into the house. A warm hand would rest on her head, a kind of benediction, while a man and his wife would argue, the woman declaring that Fionnuala was more like her father while he would say she had her mother's eyes. In the end they would seat her at the fire and bring her a tall glass of lemonade and a plate of biscuits or cake. For a while she was uncomfortable, afraid of making noise with the biscuits or that she'd slurp the drink. But she soon found that here there was nobody to watch how she behaved and to criticise her or correct her. Now and again someone would look at her and smile, but for the most part they were listening to her father's stories about where he had been, whom he had met and what they had said. He could imitate anybody's voice. They listened and laughed and prompted him to tell them more. After a long time he would remember what he had come for and they would go out to search the sheds for the implements he needed. When they heard what he was undertaking they said it would be no bother to him, of course, but they didn't pursue the subject and instead went on to ask if they'd wait for tea. Diffidently they'd enquire if Eileen was well and he'd reply that she would have come with him only her sister was supposed to call. These were the people among whom he had grown up. Some of them were related to him and had visited the house, mostly at Christmas. But they were ill-at-ease with his wife who always tried to entertain them more stylishly that they would pretend to.

108

They had stayed longer than they had meant to. The light had been turned on, but when they came outside, the sky was still bright. They'd make one more call, he said. He had been wrong to think he'd get everything done in the one day, but he'd get around to the others before the week was out.

They arrived home after ten o'clock. There was no light in the house. The sitting-room door was open and Eileen was sitting by the fire. She barely turned her head towards them. "I thought it was the squad car," she said, "coming to tell me. . . ."

He laughed at her and switched on the light. "Were we ever yet brought home dead to you!" he asked. She looked beyond him, lickering her eyes shut, closing him out. "Well, Miss," she said to Fionnuala, "and how do you think you're going to get up for school in the morning! Come here to me." And while Fionnuala stood by her chair, she unpinned the badge on her coat. She cast the spray of shamrock into the coal scuttle and laid the badge, a golden harp on a green ribbon, on the mantelpiece. "Now, get on to bed this instant." She pushed her away from her. Her father helped her out of her coat, and said they couldn't have come home and not have waited to drown the shamrock. But that never helped. "And hang up your good coat," her mother called, and as Fionnuala went upstairs she heard her telling him that he wouldn't be happy till he had some of the children as bad as himself.

Work began on the new house during the following week. In another week John and Brian were home for the Easter holidays. Every time either of them came near the house, his mother would waylay him to enquire how they were getting on and what stage were they at now. "Do you think he knows," she'd ask without faith or hope, "do you think he knows what he's at!" "He doesn't," John would confirm, "but sure I'm teaching him." And Brian would console her that the worst it could do was fall.

But day by day the house took shape. People called in to look it over. They were impressed, and agreed that he was making a fine job of it.

"Of course," her father said when they had all expressed their admiration, "it's not a perfect job. And won't be. Another man began it. And when you build from another man's foundations, you can't do as you'd like. The real right thing to do now would be to knock it and start from scratch again and do it according to your own methods." His wife shrieked at him to learn once and for all time to leave well enough alone. He ignored her and explained to his listeners that of course if a man had a woman behind him who believed in him he could embark on such things. But when your best schemes were greeted with hostility and mistrust, what could you do! It was compromise all along the line when you couldn't do it as your instinct told you it ought to be done, but had to accommodate your partner without selling your soul. It was no easy task.

"You know," they'd tell her mother afterwards, "there's a genius lost in that man. But then he could always do anything he turned his hand to. Let him see it done once and he's away."

"Oh, he can do it, all right," she'd concede now. "But the problem is to get him to do it. And then when he does start, to keep him at it."

It was only to their most trusted neighbours she would say this. And they would look away, shaking their heads. They could see the cause of her complaints. They knew too that his finest qualities were of no benefit to her, and his popularity only alienated her from both him and his friends. They recognised in him the deep-rooted malaise that made him unable to commit himself to work day after day without glory and then be deemed to have done no more than his duty. They knew how futile were her efforts to harness his skills for her own purposes. To make them feel worse they liked her too, and admired her for being proud and capable. But there was no way they could reconcile their regard for her with their instinctive understanding of him and his needs.

Then it began to rain. Her father said there wasn't much more they could do until the roof was on and it would be

110

as well to leave it. Punchestown races were on and he thought if Dick and Peter were going he might go with them. When he had gone her mother said, well it *was* Punchestown, and really she dreaded no place only Tralee. But whenever he went to Tralee she would say that at least it wasn't as bad as Galway; or Listowel; or Leopardstown; whatever crowd he met up with there, he seemed to go to hell altogether.

He was away from Tuesday till Saturday. A hundred times that week her mother would stop at the window to look down at the rough, unfinished building. And every time she'd say the same thing: that they might as well forget it, they were never going to have a new house. The blocks were dark with rain; the window spaces were like eyeless cavities in a skull and the uncovered timbers of the roof touched like pious fingertips in prayer, undefended against this first onslaught of bad weather.

On Thursday evening the rain stopped. Over the following days the sunshine steadied and strengthened. The new walls dried out again and when the work was resumed this time there were no more setbacks. The roof was on; most of the remaining work was on the inside. Her father, working on his own now, discouraged visitors, and they could no longer judge what progress was made from day to day. When they did get inside at last, one week-end when Joan and Anne-Marie were home, they were gratified to find how much had been completed and how well it was beginning to look. The kitchen bore a reassuring resemblance to kitchens they had studied in magazines. It seemed that her mother had imagined that, left to himself, her father would choose fittings so archaic, or having got the kind she wanted would instal them in such an eccentric arrangement that all who saw it would be bereft of suitable comment. But everything was precisely as she had desired it.

"Well, does that satisfy you!" he asked, coming in behind them from the sitting room. He had a trowel in one hand and in the other a board with a pat of blackened cement. Caught off guard, she laughed into his face. "Oh, sure it's lovely," she replied. "Perfect. I never knew you had it in you." "Aye," he said. His voice was cool, his look narrowed as he watched her. He noted the soft beam of approval in her eyes these days and it made him very quiet. "I saw a lovely yellow vinyl paper in the Shopping Centre. I think it might be nicer than paint. What would you say!" He told her she could paste the stars and stripes on it so long as she gave the plaster time to dry out first. He turned away. She followed him back into the sitting room. "What are you at in here!" she was asking. "Oh."

He stood aside.

She folded her arms and she chewed her lip. "The fireplace," she stated. The fireplace worried her, whilst for him it was the proudest feature of the house. He had designed it himself and built it from pieces of granite. It was the origin of the stone which, while seeming to him to be poetically apt, embarrassed her. For years two granite pillars had stood at the entrance to their old house. One of them had been knocked over when they were bringing in a digger to clear a site for the silo. For a long time it lay where it had fallen, while her mother intermittently suggested that if he had no intention of re-erecting it, then he should knock the other one too. Now he had done this and used the pieces to build the fireplace. He thought how content he would be to spend his nights at home in future if he could have his friends in. There would be a fire blazing in the grate. They would have a drink and they might play cards or just sit and talk about the years they had worked in England. And whenever he paused to put coal on the fire, or Dick reached down for a light for his cigarette, or Peter tapped out his pipe on the hearth, one of them would remark again on the lovely fireplace and the fine job he had made of it. His family, his wife would be there to hear him praised, his handiwork admired by men who, though they might never make or do anything themselves, knew craftsmanship when they saw it and whose accolades were but rarely awarded. Or when he was alone he could stretch his feet on the hearth and recall the essence of the summer's

112

day when, in the cool quiet shell of the new house, he had built it. His small fair daughter was standing beside him as he had worked, her hands clasped behind her back, her face still with wonder as she watched the skill with which he fitted the irregular pieces together, cementing them into place, the hollow of one against the curve of the next, until it all added up to a perfect rectangle.

Now he went down on one knee and with the point of the trowel delicately swabbed away a loose dab of cement. Leaving down the tools, he drew his thumb along one of the joinings, delving into the still malleable cement, his fingertips savouring the texture of the stone. Then he sat back on his heels. He ran his eyes over it without indulgence and it stood the test. He looked at his wife, defying her to show him some inadequacy in it. "You'd like me to go into the Creamery and buy you one ready-made!"

"Why, are you not satisfied with it yourself?" she asked hopefully. Then, seeing his face, she stirred uneasily. "It's too late for that, now," she added.

"You're right, it's too late," he said and began to clear away the things he had been working with.

But it would be months before she would begin to be reconciled to the fireplace, and then only when it had been admired and coveted by people whose opinion and taste she respected and who were unaware of its origins or her own uneasiness about it. Even then she suspected that they were trying to placate her or were patronising her. He said she was like all women, that nothing was of any value in her eyes unless it had a big price tag that she could show off.

But the unexpected spate of energy and enthusiasm was running out. The house was finished in all but a few details. One by one the boarding schools and colleges closed and her brothers and sisters – except Angela and Martin, who were working – came home for the summer holidays. Anne-Marie, Catherine and Joan would come and go all day between the old house and the new, measuring loors and walls and windows, discussing colour schemes for the rooms while their father was still working on them. They urged him on to finish the wardrobes he was building into the bedrooms and the presses for the kitchen and the book shelves in the sitting room.

Walking home early on the day her own school closed, Fionnuala saw her father's car in the town. Coming out of the betting office, he saw her and veering away from the two men who were with him, he waved to her to come and get into the car. The other men went on into Carberry's Lounge to watch the racing, while he sat into the car to drive Fionnuala home as if that had been his only reason for being in the town at that hour. He pulled up at the sweet shop opposite the boys' school and asked her what she'd like. She was still chewing Rovals when he stopped at the turn below the house and let her out, while he turned the car to hurry back to the town.

"I want to get to the Creamery before it closes, to get a few feet more of saddle board. I'm not forgetting the plugs, tell your mother if she asks. What width did we allow for the doors! Three foot three," he repeated after her. "Good girl. Did I give you back your ruler!"

When she got home, her mother asked "Who gave you sweets before your dinner again!" and walked away before she could hear the answer she already knew. "Indeed."

That was their second day in the new house. The evening before, Fionnuala had come home to find all the furniture in the yard in the sunlight. There was nothing left inside except a few old pieces too big or too worn for the new house. Her brothers went back and forth, carrying beds, chests of drawers, dressing tables. Her sisters followed with lighter pieces, chairs, cushions and crates of delph, clocks, ornaments, pictures, clothes, books, pots and pans.

"Come on," they called to her, "and bring that with you."

She picked up the fire-screen they had had to leave behind and she followed them down to the new house where her mother had her dinner ready. She sat on a tubular stool at the new round formica-covered table. The others had already had their first meal there. After all her intense interest in the building they had moved in without her. An old tea-towel was drying out on the rail of the new cooker.

Late summer nights she would lie in bed, the smell of white paint and wallpaper paste still fresh in the room; and waking in the morning she was dazzled by the sunlight. One by one all the rooms were papered and painted. New furniture was bought and the floors were carpeted or tiled. They'd sit in the sunshine, talking and making plans while they turned hems on the curtains, going in then to sew them on the machine. Everything would be done before the holidays ended. People often called in to see the house. Mostly they were couples who were planning to build, and her mother praised them for their good sense, putting a house in order first and then getting married, which was the right way to do things, she said, if people would only take time to think where they were going.

* * *

"Wasn't it well for you to get a bucket of water in Casey's," her father said. He had come home all bright-eyed and exuberant. They hadn't even heard the car, the wind was blowing so hard by then. The wind rushed into the kitchen and he had to lean against the back door to close it again. He bolted it and rubbed his hands together. "There's a night," he said gleefully, "will show who knows how to put a roof on a house. What do you say, Eileen?" She was at the table, mixing a cake for Fionnuala's tenth birthday. He put his arms around her. "Will we put bets on it?" His eyes glistened as he challenged her. But she had pushed him away. She told him it didn't require a storm to show up the flaws, and made him shut up and listen while she told him of the inconvenience she had suffered all day.

"Time was," he said, "you were prepared to follow me with a bag on your back. Now, twenty years on, you've gone so soft from easy living that you'd take me to court for having you carry a bucket of water across the road."

"Oh, never fear," she said, "I didn't do the carrying.

Your pet, there, I sent her off for it." Seeing the discomfort in his face, Fionnuala bent her head over the book on the table. Eileen watched him while she emptied a spoon of the cake mixture into the tin. "Another year," she said, wagging the spoon at him, "and I'll pack her off to a boarding school, like the others."

"That you will not," he said. "We've seen enough of boarding schools in this house. One young madam after another coming back here with her chin in the air and looking down her nose at her neighbours."

"Isn't it a pity," she said, pausing as she smoothed the top of the cake, "that the one time in your life that you express some policy for the upbringing of your children, it has to be a wrong one. If it's for the child's good, she'll go away to school, and too bad if it's not to the liking of your stalwart pals." She put in the cake, closed the oven door and wiped her hands. "But more to the point now, can you do anything about that water!"

He went out to the car for his torch. Several times he went up to the attic and to the hot press and to the bathroom, coming down again to search the kitchen, the garage, the boot of the car. All the time her mother grew more anxious.

"Is it serious! Another fistful of money to put it right, I suppose!"

"A minor thing woman, a minor thing," he said, holding up his hand for peace. "Now, try that tap." The water was back. Eileen switched on the immersion heater. "It's all very well," she grumbled as she retracted, "but a minor thing is a major thing when there's no one at hand to correct it."

Fionnuala had gone out to hold the torch for him while he turned on the water again. The wind buffeted them apart and the rain lashed their faces. He had put his hand on her shoulder as the light zig-zagged over the wet ground. "Water, water, everywhere, Nor any drop to drink." There was laughter in his voice and maybe later on he'd tell them how he had spent the day. For the moment, however, he was unsure of her, and did not take her allegiance for granted.

Bereavement

HE DREW the car into the side of the lane and switched off the engine. The red Toyota was parked in front of the house. Already Caroline and Patsy were racing each other across the yard, laughing and calling to him that Kal was inside. The sheepdog bounded ahead of them, barking wildly. As soon as he opened the car door they were upon him. The twins grabbed an arm each and began to haul him out of the car, while Flossie butted in between them, scrambled up on his knees and licked his face.

"Easy now, chicks, easy on there," he said. He spoke with the fancy accent he had picked up years ago when he spent a while in England. Now he eased his legs out of the car. Sitting sideways on the seat, he freed one arm and held up his hand in warning. "Your dad's in a delicate state and must be handled with care." He looked around for their mother. She was coming, but slowly. She and Kal were walking Anthony between them, holding a hand each. "Missus!" he called, as if her tardiness were unprecedented. "Call off the beast." She dragged the dog away and held her firmly by the collar, and when the twins had contained their exuberance, he emerged from the car, holding his tall, frail body as if it might break up in sections if knocked about.

"Well, did you sell the calves?" Kal said, smiling as she came towards him.

"Aye," her mother added faintly, "did you do well?"

"How much money did you get for them?" the twins asked.

"Woman!" he said. "And in front of the mites, too! Look at them!" He turned away from the signs of incipient materialism in their mint-bright eyes.

"Now," he said, flapping his hands until they all stood

117

back and left him room to move about. "Let me see, what did I bring home!" He reached into the car and brought out a parcel and looked at it this way and that, as if he couldn't remember what was in it, or how it could be opened. Giving it into their waiting hands, he turned to search among the odds and ends on the back seat. It was, as always, strewn with bits of hardware, tools, spare parts for machinery, things he bought new or second-hand whenever he came across them, knowing that even if he never used them himself, someone was bound to need them sometime. But finding nothing there that might be offered as a gift now, he eased himself out of the car again. His blue eyes were sorrowful, absorbing the meagreness of his own generosity. "I thought I had more," he said, feeling the pockets of his coat. "Aye, that's for your mother for the tea." He redeemed the half-scalped parcel and passed it on to her. Out of his pockets he scooped two fistfuls of sweets, in bars and rolls and packets. Glad to have more to offer, he was immediately distressed to find that they were ready to take the lot for themselves. He raised one hand out of reach. "We mustn't forget the other little ones. So many little ones," he said, looking around. Danny was lurking near Kal's car. Dominic was out on the road, probably looking for a lift into Carlow. At first he had pretended not to see his father getting out to open the gates, but at the last moment he had turned and come down the road to ask him for money. He had given Dominic the money, not asking either what he wanted it for nor how he had planned to get by without it, knowing well the evasive answers he'd be given.

"Sometimes I dream," he said to Kal. "I dream about mouths. They're all wide open and they're always empty and it's up to me to fill them. If I take a rest they're still there when I get up again. And then, as often as not, I find there's an extra mouth." He placed his emptied hands on the twins' heads and eased the girls one by one out of his path. "And sometimes there are two extra mouths. Tell me, do you ever have dreams like that!"

"Not about empty mouths, no," she said, trying to

smile for him.

"Are you here long before me?"

"An hour or two. I was getting ready to go again. I thought you mightn't get back till midnight, or when you had the money spent!"

"Those days are over, girl. And what'd take you off like that, on the minute. Here, wouldn't you eat a bit of Butter Scotch?" he said, giving her a small packet. "You used to be very fond of it."

He put his arm across her shoulders and led her back towards the house. There was always a delicate sick-room fragrance of port wine about him when he was dressed up. The others had already gone in and they followed them slowly around to the back door.

"You'll have to come some day I'm here," he said. "A fine day, and we could go over the place together. It must be a long time since you walked the fields." He looked down at her knee-high suede boots. "We'd have to fix you up with a pair of Wellingtons first, though. Tell me, do you have any call for them where you are?"

"Not so far," she said.

"No," he said as if he might have thought it out for himself. "No woman in that house ever had to turn a hand outside."

"Well, I wouldn't mind," she assured him.

"You would not," he agreed. "You were never afraid of work. You often gave Simon and Joe a run for their money. I can see you still," he said. The evening was cool but there was a smoky blue haze over the fields and he was reluctant to go in. They had walked as far as the gate of the paddock. "I can see you still, down on your knees, thinning turnips." They had often been out at daybreak and had trailed home at eight o'clock on a summer's evening. "They were the good days. The younger ones aren't prepared to do it. Joe can't reach on everything. He's gone back to the factory now for the season, working all the hours he can get, and who's to blame him. Well, we'll only have to work on as we are for the time being." They turned back for the house.

"No word from Simon, I suppose?"

"No," he said. "No." He knew that there never would be, but she unsettled his mind every time she came back, like a restless spirit haunting the place, seeking to reassure herself that they could manage without her. "We heard first he was on the ships and then again in Australia, so you wouldn't know. . . ." For a moment they were silent. "Tell me," he said then, "how are you getting on with Jezebel?" Up to the time of Kal's marriage, he had been on first name terms with Alice Power. He still was and in his eyes she was a fine, good-looking woman whom he had always admired and who, in turn, had always appreciated his company. But as Kal's mother-in-law she had to be considered in a new light.

"Give her no footing," he advised Kal, but he said it with some reluctance. It seemed to him that he had spent much of his life sadly listening to tales of family conflict. His sadness was for him as much as for the people involved, because he had been an only child of elderly parents and had grown up in this isolated place, craving companionship.

They had stoked up the fire and put on more briquettes. They brought him his dinner which had been kept warm in the oven. He said he had more than he could eat and left aside several slices of the smoked bacon so that they could make a sandwich each. When they had made a pot of strong tea, the parcel was opened and the cake was prodded and admired, and then divided among them. He sat the baby on his knee and managed to eat with only a fork. Neither the Mart nor the money from the sale of the calves was mentioned again.

At the far side of the room stood an old upright piano which he had bought for Kal at an auction years ago. That had been another Fair Day, and both he and the piano had been delivered at the door late that night, the only time in his life he had ever been drunk. And yet, whenever he was away his wife assumed that he had been drinking, and instead of realising that she was mistaken, she was simply resigned, satisfied that she was able to cope with the problem. Now she sat on the hearth-stool, cradling a cup of tea in her hands. Her skin seemed pink and clear, the fine lines and wrinkles smoothed away in the kind half-light. Her light brown hair was almost straight again as the permanent wave fizzled out at the ends. Kal was arranging to call for her on Saturday to take her to the hairdresser. At first she had said it would do her for another while; she'd have to get it done for Lucy's wedding anyway, but then whether amused or embarrassed because the others had stopped to listen, she had given in. Now she gazed into the heart of the fire, reassured by the familiar background of noise in the room, her husband and children argueing, joking and making the baby laugh and squeal. Meanwhile, outside the isolated house on this evening in late March, the light died out of the land, out of the fallow fields. The harsh long winter and the late spring had delayed the sowing. Across the boundary of their fields the still leafless branches and twigs of the trees were pencil-sketched against the sky. Someone switched on the light and drew the curtains.

Their father was driving the twins berserk telling them that he had met all their teachers in the town that day and the things he had said to them.

"And the big nun said that Caroline was very good at her Apologetics, and I told her. 'Well ma'am, I'm glad. . . .'"

"You shouldn't call her ma'am, she's Sister."

"Is that it? That must have been why the little nun was nudging her and smirking. Well, anyway, I told her I was glad to hear it but then we had always seen to it that they had manners at home and to say they were sorry if they did anything out of the way."

"Lord, Daddy, it's not that at all. They'll think you're awful ignorant." She looked around, appealing to them all to see how he was ruining her reputation in school. But nobody cared. They were all laughing and then she began to laugh too, linking her arm in his and pounding his back with her fist. "Anyway you couldn't have because we don't learn Apologetics."

"Oh it's a fact," he said, "and they were two grand women, mind you."

"I hope you didn't call them women to their face," she said.

"And why wouldn't I! 'Begor ma'am,' says I, 'you're a fine figure of a woman to be a nun. Isn't it a pity to have the likes of you in a convent and all the poor divils that are mad looking for a wife!' "

'Patsy, are you listening! Mammy, I'm never going to school again if he did."

"Oh, indeed I did. And she was glad to hear it, what's more. She threw back her head and laughed and gave me a slap on the chest. Nearly knocked me over, there in the middle of the street, and everyone stopping to look at us. 'And that's a grand little lump of a girl you have there with you, too,' I remarked. 'You're a pair, I'll be bound, wouldn't say no to a little refreshment. So if you care to accompany me, I was just on my way into the Corner House, here.' And do you think they refused! 'Set them up there, Pat,' says I to young Dwyer. 'A drop of port for myself and two pints, I believe, for my chums.' 'Go on in there to the snug,' says he, trying to pretend he didn't notice them, 'and I'll attend to you right away.' 'Snug Not at all,' says the big lady. 'We'll have them here at the bar where there's a bit of crack.' And she hitched up the long skirt and hoisted herself onto a high stool next to this big cattle-dealer from Tipperary."

He pushed aside his plate. "Now," he said to Patsy, "is there a cup of tea left for your father! You cleared the cake between you, I suppose."

"I have a slice here for you," his wife said. He cut up his share of the cake so that the younger ones all had another mouthful. "Now," he said, moving away from the table and handing the baby over to Kal, "how about a few bars of music. Danny" And like a genie, Danny appeared at his side with the accordion. While he settled it on his knee and hitched the strap onto his shoulder, his wife had begun to tidy the table, but without insistance.

She left down the bundle of knives and spoons she had collected, pushed the cups and saucers in from the edge of the table and sat down again.

The music broke off for a moment. "The cows!" her husband enquired, raising his head. "They're not milked, I suppose!"

"No, we hadn't got around to them yet,"

"Aye, well, they were late milking this morning," he said, his fingers touching the keys again. "They'll hold out another while. What are we going to play now, anyone! It's a long time, I suppose," he said to Kal, "since you heard the Rocks Of Bawn played!" The song had been going through his mind all day, tugging at dormant memories, and then he had come home to find Kal here.

But now everything had changed and when the sound of the motor-cycle roared into the yard, drowning every other sound, that was the end of their music. Chairs were moved around to make room for another two, and more briquettes were put on the fire as Lucy and Tommy Nugent came in.

"Well, what were you playing!" Tommy enquired, when they had settled down at the fire. "Go on, I'd like to hear it."

"We were finished," Patsy said. She had taken the accordion and was fastening it to put it away, though her mother might look wistfully apologetic as if she felt that one of them ought to play him a tune since he asked. Her father, embarrassed at finding himself empty-handed, said it was time he went to milk the cows. But he made no move until Kal said it was time she went home, she had never intended staying so late and Michael wouldn't know where she had gone.

It was dark when they came outside and an ice-cold breeze whipped around the corner of the house. The yard light was broken and her father sent Danny back to the kitchen for a torch, but she knew he wouldn't come back, so she went on ahead to turn on the car lights.

"Lucy and Tommy will go with you as far as the end of the lane," he said, trying still to orchestrate the hospitality of the entire family. "They'll open the gates for you."

But she insisted on going alone. She remembered how he used to delegate her, and the others too, to run the most superfluous errands for visitors. The buckle on Lucy's shoe caught the light as she pressed Tommy's foot, warning him to stay where he was.

"I'll be all right," Kal said. "I can manage."

Even as she turned the car, her father directing her, they had all gone in again. Out on the lane she stopped to adjust the seat which some of them had moved. Her father was still standing there, lonely and beleaguered as a tree in the wind, waiting until she started the car again. The last she saw of him he was walking back towards the sheds where his wife had rigged up a lantern and was getting set to help him with the milking.

A Minor Incident

THE ARMY truck had passed them earlier on the road. The driver had kept close to the edge, forcing them to pull the prams onto the grass verge, to press back against the hedge until the briars pricked their shoulders. The covered truck passed so close to them, looming above them, that the children cried with fright. Then it was gone. Shaken, they stepped out into the road again. From the back of the truck the soldiers grinned.

Captain barked as he raced along on the other side of the hedge. He had broken away from them earlier and now he rushed back to the sound of the motor, scrambling through a gap to shake himself and bark at the truck. But it was too far off by then and when Sara shouted to him, he gave up and came back to her. He squatted in front of her, still panting, his pink tongue rippling between the white rows of spiky teeth, his bushy tail swishing clouds of dust off the road. He blocked her way until she patted him and talked to him, and then he fell in behind and followed tamely for another while.

They had walked too far in the heat and now on the way home Sara lagged behind the others. Her mother and Mrs. Martin walked on in front, pushing their prams. Mrs. Flynn stooped to lift up her child. He had stumbled again and dropped his bottle of milky tea and she would have to carry him the rest of the way. She was going to have another baby soon. Her leg was bandaged. Her hair kept on falling in around her face and when she was out of earshot Mrs. Martin would whisper about her until she caught up with them again. When their own baby awoke, Sara's mother sat him up and lifted Mrs. Flynn's child onto the end of the pram.

As they walked on, back over the bridge and around the

turn, they hurried towards the shade of the tall trees that grew on either side of the road, the branches meeting overhead. Here they lingered, feeling kinder towards each other. The river slurped against the arch of the bridge and when they moved on they could hear inside the walls of the estate the sharp rap back and forth of a tennis ball. They followed the staccato rhythm of the game and heard the voices of the Corbetts and their friends who were spending the summer there. As they passed the green door in the wall through which they might see the lawns, the tennis court, the shrubbery and the glasshouses, Mrs. Flynn winked at Sara to come and peep too, but her mother had turned around and was beckoning her to come on. They were out on the open road again, with low banks on either side topped by barbed wire fences, when they heard the distant sound of an engine on the road behind them. Sara's mother and Mrs. Martin looked at each other.

"They're coming back," Mrs. Flynn said. "Come on, quick, we'll be as far as your house."

"Oh, it might not be them at all," Sara's mother said. But she reached back and grabbed Jamie's hand and he trotted along beside her, looking back, and stumbling. "Sara!" she turned to her and smiled. "That dog, is he gone again? Oh well, he's probably home by now."

They were hurrying towards Martins' house when the truck came roaring down the road behind them and Captain reappeared, darting out under the wire. They had just reached the beginning of the privet hedge that sheltered the front of the house from the road and were walking in single file on the grassy margin.

The truck drove up beside them, the wheels spewing clouds of dust, and Captain came running after it, barking at the rolling wheels and at the men in the back of the truck who were yelling at him. Mrs. Flynn called Captain to come back. The truck braked suddenly and Captain too skidded to a halt behind it. He crouched there, yapping at the jeering men as they pelted him with small stones and pellets of hardened mud they picked off the floor of the truck. He whimpered when they hit him and would cower for a moment. But he would not stay away. Mrs. Flynn and Sara caught him between them and tried to coax him and lead him away. And all the time the engine churned the stillness of the day to shreds. Mrs. Flynn held him back, her arms binding him against her legs while he struggled, quivering and panting with excitement, to escape. Mrs. Martin whispered to Sara's mother that they should all go into the house. "Maybe they won't mind us," she said. But her mother shook her head and stayed there. She was trying to soothe Jamie and Mrs. Flynn's child who had begun to cry.

"Come on, let him out, Missus," one of the men shouted to Mrs. Flynn. He was sitting nearest to the opening, facing them. He held his rifle across his knees. Mrs. Flynn tightened her arms around the dog and looked to the other women. "Come on, Missus, let him off." He swivelled around, resting on one knee, the rifle against his shoulder. The other soldiers looked on, and the driver rested his elbow on the ledge of the window and adjusted the mirror.

Then another soldier poised his rifle, grinned and said, "Leave him to me, I can take him where he is." But the first soldier pushed him aside with his elbow. He shrugged his shoulders and sat back. Sara searched all their faces. There was one soldier, a thin pale man with a dark moustache, who sat there with his hands clasped between his knees. He looked on with none of the anticipation of the others, but neither with impatience, as if all this had been bound to occur and he must bide while it lasted.

"Ah, what do you want with the poor dog," Mrs. Flynn said. She smirked as she glanced at the other women to see what they thought, and to blame their presence if her tactics were not the most effective she might have used. "He belongs to the little one here. Sure you wouldn't harm him."

The soldier with the moustache stretched his leg, turned away and looked across the flat countryside. It was to him Sara felt they should have appealed to stop it. Now she too turned away. She stood there waiting, her head bowed, her fingers twisting the fringe of the baby's sun shade. She heard the soldier saying, in his alien accent, "Maybe you'd rather I'd shoot him where he is . . . take two birds. . . ." She heard them whispering and someone laughed. "Three birds, aye. What do you say, Missus?"

Mrs. Flynn's arms went limp. The truck began to trundle away from them. Captain slipped from her arms. He stood still for a moment, unsure of his freedom. But as the truck picked up speed, he streaked away after it again, barking excitedly, flurries of dust in his wake. The soldier aimed and fired, and fired and fired again until the barking stopped. And when Sara looked up, the truck was near the top of the hill, clouded in dust as it gathered speed. The soldier was still shooting, into the air now, every shot puncturing the fragile blue shell of the day. Frightened birds flew squawking out of the hedges and trees, and in Martins' paddock a mare and her foal left their grazing and ran to the far side and the stamping of their hooves vibrated along the hard ground. And when the noise had stopped and the dust cleared she saw Captain lying on the road at the foot of the hill, unbelievably still as they approached him. Blood oozed through his brown and white coat in darkening patches and trickled onto the road and was absorbed in the dust.